Jungles Long Ago

Jungles Long Ago

KENNETH ANDERSON

RUPA

First published in 2002 by
Rupa Publications India Pvt. Ltd.
7/16, Ansari Road, Daryaganj
New Delhi 110002

Sales centres:
Allahabad Bengaluru Chennai
Hyderabad Jaipur Kathmandu
Kolkata Mumbai

Fifth impression 2012

ISBN: 978-81-716746-5-7

10 9 8 7 6 5

Typeset by
Mindways Design
1410 Chiranjiv Tower
43 Nehru Place
New Delhi 110 019

Printed in India by
Gopsons Papers Ltd.
A-14 Sector 60
Noida 201 301

Contents

Introduction

AMONG THE PLEASURES OF WRITING BOOKS ARE THE LETTERS THAT often come to an author from readers all over the world. Some of them are highly flattering and add to the writer's vanity as they record the hours of enjoyment derived from his stories. A few ask questions and demand an early answer, while others seek to put the author on the spot in one way or the other.

Recently I received a letter from England in which I was asked why I preach animal preservation in nearly all my books, while most of my stories are about shooting them. But I feel that most of my readers will believe and understand me when I say that I have never killed for pleasure, at least not since I was very young. I do plead guilty for the sins of my youth; but the urge to slay wantonly died in me comparatively early; since then I have been able to kill only in cases of necessity.

Due to something I once told Malcolm Barnes, my publisher, which he included in his foreword to my last book, Tales of the Indian Jungle, I have received many letters urging me to continue writing, if for no other reason than to increase public interest in the jungles and the wild life that remains in India. So I have decided to try to do just that, but in this new book there are no stories of shooting man-eaters, or of shooting anything for that matter. Instead, you will find reminiscences of adventures in the jungle a long time ago. Some of the things we did then were pointless; some were just crazy and I would not have the guts to undertake them again today, now that I am, I hope, a wiser man. And there is a chapter on occult lore and another on jungle medicine.

All these reminiscences are jewels in a long chain of memories; precious jewels that sparkle for me brightly as I gaze at each and remember it once again, reliving those wonderful days and nights when we passed each exciting moment so happily, so fully, with never a thought of the what-might-have-happened or what-might-happen. The present was all that mattered and we lived each moment to the full.

Those were the times when there were no problems, no frustrations, no anxieties for the future. We were of and in the jungle, and that was all that mattered—with the trees and the animals and the sunshine about us in the daytime, and the moon and the stars and the fireflies, the croaking of frogs and the chirping of the crickets by night, we were in a paradise of contentment, the calls of frightened deer and the chorus of a pack of jackals were the music to which we fell asleep beside the embers of our fires, stoked now and again by the one whose turn it was to be on 'sentry-go', so to speak, as he added a bunch of faggots or a small log, when the sparks would leap skywards, pursued by a billow of smoke.

Camp life was relaxing in every sense of the word; but we were strict, very strict, about the duties of the 'sentry' for two hours, which was the length of time each of the party was obliged to spend in protecting the camp, and for which we cast lots the evening before.

The 'sentry' was required to stoke the fire and keep his senses alert for the approach of elephants, particularly of a single bull. Also to listen to the sounds and cries of the night, from which his comrades would be able to learn what had happened in the forest while they slept. The offender who was caught dozing at his post not only became the butt of caustic comment, but was compelled to do a double duty the following night.

So imagine now that you are seated before this fire. You are in a glade of a great forest; towering trees surround you, clothed in a cloak of blackness broken by a thousand sparklers, the myriad tropical fireflies. Close your eyes and listen to my tales of tigers, of adventure and mystery, as the jungle breezes waft the night scent of the wild flowers on a cool current that fans your brow, and remember that you are in a land where time is of no consequence and the word 'hurry' is never spoken.

One

A Night in Spider Valley

ERIC NEWCOMBE, WHO FIGURES SO LARGELY IN THIS STORY, WAS AT school with me. We were great friends, and one of the reasons for this was that Eric had a very pretty sister.

Unfortunately, he was one of those people occasionally encountered who have an inevitable attraction for trouble. To make my meaning clear, if you were with Eric you could surely expect something unfortunate to happen. It was almost a certainty.

Sometime, as boys, we raided orchards, or we raided the girls' school at night, dressed as ghosts or Red Indians, or the dormitories of the convent, running the gauntlet of the nuns a dozen times; yet we always escaped, except when Eric was with us. For we tried it all again with him in the party. Dressed as 'yoemen' of old—Eric was 'Guy Fawkes', I remember— we had once terrified the girls in their beds at the convent and were making good our escape, pursued by various nuns

1

with umbrellas, but vaulting over the wall to freedom, at whose feet do you think we fell? None other than our own headmaster, returning from a late night about which he was careful not to speak.

Eric was such a bumpkin that, not content with falling in love with a girl whose parents strongly disapproved, he had to fall off the wall he had climbed over in order to see her and to break his arm in the process. And when we were in pursuit of 'The Killer of Jalahalli', a panther that had been wounded, whose story I have already told* Eric, who was with me, had to go and get himself mauled. Not long afterwards we visited a circus and Eric conceived the idea of stroking a panther in its cage. As might have been expected, the panther resented this familiarity and badly clawed his hand. I might mention that for both of these catastrophies I got all the blame from his wife, for he had married that girl some years after falling off the wall.

Then one night we went to shoot wild pig at Gulhatti. It poured with rain. We were sitting in a field for the pig, but I decided to give up and return to the forest bungalow. But not Eric. What was a little rain after all, he asked? He would bag a pig regardless. He got pneumonia instead, and his wife blamed me even for that!

I have told you about these incidents so that you might appreciate that I was not overenthusiastic when this Jonah suggested we do a night jaunt into the jungle in search of adventure. To ensure we met with excitement in some shape or form, he stressed we should go unarmed but should carry torches and a supply of food. That was something at least. He was such a crazy character that I would not have been

* See: *Nine Man-Eaters and One Rogue.*

surprised it the least had he made it mandatory that we went torchless and foodless as well.

Eric was very likeable, extremely persuasive, very fond of nature and the wild, quite unassuming and altogether irresponsible. He was quite unaware of the possible trouble that some of his actions could bring to him and his unfortunate companions. I am always game for an adventure, but when I realised it was to be in the company of this amiable character, I do confess I felt a considerable degree of doubt.

Those of you who have read of my adventures with the tiger I have called 'The Novice of Manchi'* and my earlier story about 'The Marauder of Kempekerai',** will remember the valley I have described in those stories and which I called 'Spider Valley'. It is a deep and densely forested valley in the district of Salem, extending southward for about twenty miles from a little hamlet named Aiyur and enclosed between two lofty mountain ranges.

This valley is the bed of a stream, and a narrow footpath accompanies the stream, crossing it every now and then as the stream turns to right and left in an attempt to shorten the overall distance. The mountain ranges to west and east tower above the valley bottom, sometimes oppressively close, giving the traveller the impression that he is in a leafy tunnel. A delightful forest lodge, known as the Kodekarai bungalow, on the slopes of the Gutherayan peak at a height of over 4,000 feet, and to the east of the valley, overlooks the scene as the stream and the valley struggle onward to their ultimate junction ten miles away with the Chinar river, itself a tributary of the great Cauvery river, which is the biggest in south India.

---

* See: *The Tiger Roars.*
** See: *Man-Eaters and Jungle Killers.*

We chose 'Spider Valley' for *ghoom* (a Hindustani word signifying to 'wander' or 'stroll') for a variety of reasons. It was a very densely forested area and abounded in those days with elephant, bison, tiger, panther and bear. Sambar and jungle-sheep, rather than spotted deer, were plentiful because of the hilly terrain and adjacent mountain ranges. Rock snakes, commonly termed pythons, were said to be present in numbers, and smaller animal life was abundant. The tall, waving bamboos and the damp undergrowth were the home of millions of fireflies as well as of a luminiscent beetle and three varieties of 'glow-worm'. Finally, I knew it to be the only area in Salem district where, by virtue of the dampness of the evergreen jungle, a hamadryad (king cobra) might be encountered.

In those early days I owned a fleet of Model T Fords, thirteen of them at one time in fact and all in running order. Purchased at various military auctions as scrap at prices ranging from Rs. 50/- to Rs.250 (£2.50 to £12.50), I tinkered with them and put them back upon the road for use on my trips to the jungle. The cheapest buy was an engine on its chassis and wheels for Rs.12 (about 60p.). Upon this chassis I fixed a body consisting of a dual-purpose box *machan* that could be rigged up on a tree or placed over a hole dug in the earth. Handles helped to fix this *machan* to a tree, while loopholes in the sides provided apertures for firing when it was employed to cover a pit dug in the ground. The whole contraption, as I have indicated, was clamped to the chassis of the model to form an inverted compartment in which to carry my tools, food, water and bedding. A comfortable cane chair, secured over the petrol tank, made a fine driving-seat. As for mudguards, there were none. Nor a windshield. A pair of dark glasses served to keep the grit out of my eyes.

It is true I was covered with dust by journey's end, or bespattered with mud on a rainy day, but this added to the fun. A companion, if there was one, would be seated on a similar cane chair to my left, and I would delight in driving the left front wheel of this vehicle very skilfully through pools of rainwater or heaps of cowdung, and laugh when he was showered with mud or worse.

Eric had a great liking for this vehicle which he called 'Sudden Death' and was adamant that we should make our journey in it, or rather on it, which would be a truer term, in preference to any of the other Model Ts.

I must tell you that it was, and still is, against the law to travel about on a chassis as a regular means of transport. The law requires that there must be a regular body of some sort on any vehicle. The question of registering 'Sudden Death' and obtaining a number for it had therefore to be solved. You will remember it was sold as scrap and had no number at the time. So I removed the numberplate from one of my other Model Ts and drove that vehicle down to the registration office for the needful action. On the application form that had to be filled in was entered both the engine number and chassis number of 'Sudden Death'. The engine and chassis numbers of the vehicle used as a substitute were doctored with a coating of shellac which made them indecipherable; it could be removed later by scraping and a few drops of petrol. 'Sudden Death' was duly registered and given a new number. That, too, under its very own engine and chassis serial numbers. The law was powerless after that to prosecute me for driving about on a chassis that did not have a regular body, for the portable *machan* could not officially be regarded as such. The car that had been presented in its place resumed its own identity when its own number was put back after the shellac coating had been removed.

There were two other features about 'Sudden Death' which I have still to record. The first was that I have fitted

5

it with a special carburettor—also picked up as scrap—which enabled me to start the engine on petrol, and switch to kerosene when it had heated up. A Model T. covered about twenty-four miles to the gallon. Petrol in those days cost fourteen *annas* per gallon (about £0.05), and kerosene 8 *annas* a gallon, or about half the price. So motoring on kerosene was economical indeed. Engine oil was 3½ Rs. or £0.20 a gallon, while brand new tyres were around Rs. 15 or £0.70 each.

The other feature of 'Sudden Death' was a Ruxtel back axle. This provided a very low and a very high gear, in addition to the two transmission gears operated by pedal on every Model T. 'Sudden Death' could, therefore, because of her 22 hp engine and light weight almost climb a wall, and on the flat she could nip along under kerosene at a speed that made many a new car look like a tortoise. As for a failing spark plug, I never bothered to carry a spare. Pending cleaning it when I had the time to do so, all that was required was removal from the cylinder head, for 'Sudden Death' would then snort along on three cylinders as if she had never had a fourth!

As we would be on the move all night, we planned to wear the lightest clothing, the proverbial khaki, while I donned the pair of knee-length, alpaca-lined, rubber-soled boots that I generally wore on such prowls. They are light, noiseless and soft, but thick enough to absorb the fangs of any Russell's viper or a cobra that might be lurking in the undergrowth and inadvertently stamped upon. Eric wore rubber-soled boots with the ends of his pants tucked into them. Snakes offer the greatest hazard at night, far greater than that of running into an elephant or a bear. Tigers and panthers, unless man-eaters, wounded or in the act of mating, offer practically no danger at all.

'Sudden Death' took us to the Aiyur Forest Lodge without incident. Here we had dinner. Then, carrying our food and a change of clothing in haversacks upon our backs, and a bag of spare torch-cells each, we set forth for Spider Valley, the best part of three miles away. I had a five-cell torch hanging in a cloth case at my side while I used a three-cell torch, handier for spotting. Eric carried a pair of three-cell torches. There is a fire-line leading through the forest in a southeasterly direction from the lodge. After nearly a mile this traverses the edge of a water hole, then changes direction westwards and after some time meets a track leading up a hill to another forest lodge at a place named Gulhatti.

At this water hole we had our first adventure. Our torches revealed a row of twin-pointed green lights on the opposite bank of the pool which kept bobbing up and down restlessly in an attempt to escape the unwinking stare of our torch-beams. A herd of spotted deer had been caught in the act of drinking!

I sank to my haunches to watch them, but Eric left the *path* we were following and moved down towards the water. This was a mistake, for his clothing got caught in the wait-a-bit thorns that clustered around the pool. Apart from scratching himself, he made quite a lot of noise and made yet another mistake. He moved into the beam from my torch, thereby revealing to the deer that the bright objects they had been staring at all this while, but could not quite identify, were connected with their deadliest enemy—man. With a drumming of hooves the herd disappeared like magic. But a far more ominous sound took its place.

'Woof! Woof! Woof!' A bear had come down to drink. And he, too, had done the unexpected thing.

He must have been moving along the very pathway we had been following and had decided to drink. So he went down to the pool just ahead of Eric. Being hard of hearing and poor of sight, the bear did not hear us at first, nor notice our torch-beams. Maybe he had his head down and was

7

drinking. But when Eric began to crash about and show himself in my light, and the spotted deer thundered away in alarm, the bear realised that something was cooking and that something was directly behind him.

Like all his kind when they get alarmed, he did not wait to think. It did not even occur to him to run away. Instead, he rushed headlong at the intruder. Time enough for him to find out the nature of the intruder later. So he charged straight at Eric at top speed, and Eric at the moment was caught in the wait-a-bit thorns!

What did he do at this critical moment! He hurled his three-cell torch straight at the oncoming bear, then only a few feet away. Only he could have done such a thing.

Here was a bear coming hell for leather at the light when—behold!—the light came hell for leather at him! By luck the torch struck Bruin somewhere in the face, with the result that, as quickly as he had made up his mind to charge, he now made up his mind to run away. Veering to his left he disappeared in a crashing of bushes and loud 'Woofs!' Eric left the thorns with some of his clothing adhering there, rushed to where I stood rooted to the spot, and exclaimed 'A bear!'

I remained silent.

We turned due west for some time and then south along a much narrower track, which was the pathway we were to follow for twenty miles till it met the Chinar river. It led downhill and we entered Spider Valley. The vegetation grew densely on all sides; the lantana bushes, with their clusters of red, pink and orange-coloured flowers, visible in our torch-beams, were rapidly giving away to increasingly dense clumps of bamboo.

Then we heard the sound of elephants: a crash as one of these monsters tore down a culm of bamboo, followed by a curious 'wheenk' as the tender upper leaves and outer skins of which elephants are very fond were peeled off. Finally the thicker base stem was cast away. Truly wasteful creatures they are; for the sake of a basketful of tender leaves and skin, a whole massive culm had been destroyed.

Was this animal alone, or was there a whole herd grazing at the head of the valley for which we were making? We squatted on the ground to await further evidence, and for a while there was absolute silence. Then we heard the swishing as the elephant beat upon the ground a bunch of leaves that he had gathered at the end of his trunk preparatory to stuffing the whole lot into his mouth.

Then silence again, but not for long: 'Phutt! Phutt! Phutt! Phutt!', followed by a prolonged 'whooshing' sound.

He was closer to us than we had thought for these sounds revealed that he was answering the call of nature. It was also becoming apparent that he was probably alone.

He was directly ahead of us and the breeze was blowing from us in his direction, so that it could only be a matter of minutes, if not seconds, before he caught our scent. Then one of three things might happen.

Normally he should just have melted away into the jungle as elephants have a habit of doing, regardless of their great bulk, when they get scent of man. On the other hand he might stand absolutely still, as motionless as a rock, hoping that we might either pass him by without noticing his presence, or if he was on mischief bent, to allow us to come close enough to enable him to charge down upon us devastatingly. The third, but most improbable alternative, was to charge us without further ado. Elephants, even when in *musth* or in any other irritable mood, are unlikely to do this. The majority think things over for a minute or two before acting.

I was about to grab Eric and move off to the left to start a long detour in order to avoid the creature when a fresh

9

sound came to our ears: 'Quink! Quink! Quink!' The sound of a baby elephant nuzzling up to its mother.

We now knew we were in far less danger: unless one gets too close to such a baby, a herd will generally avoid human beings. It is the solitary elephant one has to be careful of.

At least, that was the way things ought to have gone.

But there were other factors. For one thing, it was night; for another, the beams from our torches would frighten the elephants, even annoy them. We had deliberately chosen a dark night, for although the jungle looks pleasantly ethereal in the moonlight, to move about in such light gives one's position away far sooner than in real darkness. Further, our torch-beams would not carry very far in moonlight and the reflection of the eyes of an animal would be far weaker than in pitch darkness.

We had already agreed to talk as little as possible, so I extinguished my torch and with my free hand reached out to grasp and turn off Eric's too. For a moment the darkness was intense, then as our eyes became accustomed to the gloom, the darkness softened and the glitter of the stars added considerable illumination to our surroundings.

The silence continued to be intense. It became oppressive. It got on our nerves. Eventually it became ominous as we began to feel we were being watched.

A low and continued rumbling like distant thunder came from our right. But the sky was clear and star-spangled, so the noise could not possibly herald rain. Where did it come from?

Eric was staring hard to the right as we heard the rumbling again. I could see he was a little alarmed. Finally he put his lips to my ear and asked in a whisper, 'Do you hear that? Can it be a tiger?

I raised my finger to my mouth to enjoin silence, rubbed my stomach with my other hand, and stabbed my forefinger in the direction where we had first heard the elephants. The starlight was bright enough for us to see each other and Eric recognised my action. I was trying to tell him that the rumbling sound came from the digestive processes of an elephant's stomach.

There are five fundamental lessons a night-prowler should learn if he hopes to prowl with success, whether 'ghooming' like ourselves or reconnoitring the front lines of an 'enemy'. The first is not to talk, or even whisper, on any account. The second is to 'freeze' at sight or sound of an animal or an enemy as the case may be. The third is to keep to the shadows and avoid crossing open spaces. The fourth is to be careful where you place your foot, for even if it is too dark to see, taking a false step into thorns or causing the dried leaves to rustle, will give away your position. You must cultivate the habit on these occasions of moving each foot forward in the manner of soldiers on a ceremonial slow-step parade rather than raising the knee and bringing the foot downwards, as in normal walking. Of course, this requires a little practice, but more than that it needs conscious forethought, remembering to use the 'glide-step' in a night-time *ghoom* rather than lapsing forgetfully into your ordinary walk.

The fifth and least thing to remember at all times, especially when you 'freeze', is to 'freeze' literally and not keep fidgeting about, slapping at mosquitoes, scratching, raising your hands to your face, and such-like actions.

You should never forget that the faintest whisper becomes audible in the still night air, while the slightest motion attracts the attention of an alert animal, or an enemy, as the case may be, and will give you away. Bear these five tips in mind always if you have occasion to go out on a night *'ghoom'*, or under different circumstances if you don't want to invite an enemy bullet in your direction. Eric had broken

the very first of them by whispering to me and the nearest
elephant had heard him.

An instant later there came an earth-shaking 'Tri-aa-ank!
Tri-aa-ank'—the alarm cry of a frightened female.

These huge creatures are almost unpredictable. You can
never say how they may react even under exactly similar
circumstances, though with a wide experience of them in the
wild, I can say that usually, under certain conditions, you may
expect one of them to behave in this way or that.

After that alarm call, pandemonium reigned for a short
time. Then followed a chorus of cries from all around us:
'Kakk! Kakk! Kakk!' as mothers summoned their young
peremptorily, accompanied by 'Quink! Quink! Quink!' as a
dozen baby-elephants hurried to shelter beneath their mothers'
bellies. What was more frightening was a prolonged roar from
the streambed now only a few yards in front of us.

'Ahha-a-a-a-a-ah!Ahha-a-a-a-a-ah!' A bull-elephant,
probably the master of the herd, had herd the alarm signal
of his mates; he cried his reassurance as he hurried to their
aid, while another male, this time to our left but further off
also answered with a roar. Then the first bull, coming headlong
toward us, splashed through the water. We heard the squelching
as he hurried across the stream, roaring as he came.

We were unarmed, remember, and on foot. I grabbed Eric
by the elbow. We turned and scurried back along the *path*.
No time, now, for cautious walking. Rather, we broke into
a jog trot.

Meanwhile the bull behind us, still roaring, rejoined the
females who had raised the first alarm. He had stopped
roaring now. Only the squeals and squeaks of the young and
the coughing 'Kakk! Kakk!' calls of summoning mothers
could be heard. The second bull, who had also been roaring,
had probably joined them as well, for his roars stopped too.

If either or both the bulls decided to chase us now, as likely as not they would start off in silence and only give vent to the shrieking trumpet-sound of attack when they actually saw or scented us. This would be quite different in timbre from the shrill cry of fear and alarm first voiced by the frightened cow. The attacking note is pitched higher and is more prolonged. There is no mistaking the quality of hatred, anger and menace that is put into such a sound, while the alarm-cry is lower-pitched and of shorter, quicker duration, rarely voiced more than twice in succession.

Instead, we heard crashing sounds which seemed to be receding behind us. The 'quicks' of the young had stopped. Evidently the leader had decided that discretion was the better part of valour and was taking his charges away. Now numerous splashings announced that the animals were crossing the stream. We stopped running and sat down to listen.

A few moments later complete silence reigned except for a distant 'Ponk! Ponk! Ponk!' as a sambar doe, high up on a hillside to our right, who had heard all the commotion below, decided some danger might be afoot and voiced her own alarm.

Eric brought his lips to my ear again and whispered 'what now?'

I shrugged, held up the palm of a hand to signify we should wait a little and then, by pointing my forefinger down into the valley, indicated that we would continue our journey. Eric saw my point. Having started, we were not going back just for the sake of a few elephants.

We waited perhaps fifteen minutes to allow the herd to move out of the way. Then we got up and continued our cautious progress down the valley. Very soon we reached the stream. It was perhaps twenty yards wide at this spot. The water reached almost from bank to bank, which accounted for the great amount of splashing we heard when the elephants crossed over, but it was barely knee-deep, as we found out for ourselves when we followed the *path* which cut across the stream for the first time.

The undergrowth on the farther bank was very dense. There was less lantana here and a great deal of *vellari* shrubbery in its place, while mighty trees with trunks of great girth met overhead, their branches crowding and completely obscuring the starlight. Bamboos in profusion grew in massive clumps on both banks of the stream.

The darkness was stygian and a high breeze, which had just risen, blowing down the valley from behind us, caused the bamboos to creak and groan and their culms to bend and thrash wildly against one another. This breeze was unfortunate; we did not like it at all. Coming from behind, it would spread our scent far and wide and warn the animals ahead of our approach. Carnivora have a very poor sense of smell, so it hardly mattered as far as they were concerned, but deer and elephant would know we were coming long in advance of our arrival. We would not see many of the former, while the latter, unless on mischief bent, would give us a wide berth. At the same time, the noise made by the breeze filled the air and prevented us from hearing anything else.

I walked ahead, flashing my three-cell, while Eric followed closely. I had cautioned him not to use his torch, as its beams would fall upon myself and advertise my presence. Further, the light of a second torch from behind is very distracting to the person in front, for various reasons.

The elephant herd had taken itself off in some other direction, and for the time being, at least, there was neither sight nor sound of them, although we found ample evidence of their recent presence in the valley in the form of broken branches, chewed fragments of bamboo, and huge balls of dung all over the pathway.

A moment later something sticky and clammy clung to my face. I could not see it although my torch was lit. Then I recognised what it was: I had walked into the web of one of those enormous spiders that live in large numbers in this valley, and for which reason I had called it 'Spider Valley'. These spiders are huge, often measuring as much as ten inches from leg-tip to leg-tip across the body. This one was not great in bulk, however; it was perhaps the size of a large marble. The abdomen and thorax were black with vivid stripes of yellow running around and across. The eyes were large and blood-red and reflected torchlight as if two large rubies were hanging side by side in midair. The legs were long, hairless, black and powerful, as if made of wire.

I had watched these creatures spinning their webs in daylight. They climb to a high branch and from there they let themselves drop, emitting a thread behind them. When they judge they have fallen far enough, they control any further fall by the simple expedient of not emitting further thread. In this position, head downwards, they hang till a gust of breeze blows the thread close enough to some leaf or branch, to which they immediately cling and attach the thread. If no breeze comes within an appreciable time, the spider climbs up the line of web thread by which it has descended, and tries all over again from a more advantageous position.

Having secured the first line of its thread as a sort of bridgehead, it climbs to the top of this second tree and repeats the action by dropping itself from there while adjusting the length of thread emitted from its abdomen till it meets the first line of web, to which it attaches this new strand. Waiting for the breeze again, it drops lower to reach some point a few feet off the ground and a little distance from the first tree from which it began its operation.

The spider has now spun a huge X, extending some fifteen to twenty feet across. It now returns to the point it had started from and begins to connect all four corners of the letter X to each other by running up and down the arms of the letter X until it has made a huge rectangle with the X in the centre.

The rest is simple; the spider moves around and around, weaving strands of web in parallel lines all around, and perhaps half-an-inch from each other. All this is mighty hard work, but the spider I watched one morning, just starting work on its web as I walked down this valley, had finished by the time I returned that way late the same evening: a wonderful exhibition of precision engineering for an insect of its size.

These creatures will devour anything that gets caught in their webs, butterflies, moths, beetles, and even the smaller species of birds whose blood it consumes. The strands of its webs, although no thicker than the finest thread are very elastic and incredibly strong. Even a single strand will not break easily under strain. Moreover, the substance that forms this strand is very sticky.

Once the work is done, the spider takes up its position in the centre of the web with its legs outstretched. In this position, due to its colouring, it looks like some leaf-stem or other insignificant object suspended in midair. It hangs motionless, but entirely alert. As soon as some creature flies inadvertently against the web, the sticky substance of which the strands are made adhere to it. The creature flutters and struggles, thus fouling other sticky strands.

Immediately, the spider in the middle of the web comes to life. It scurries towards its prey and scampers swiftly round and round it, emitting an endless flow of threads until the prey is entirely encased and enmeshed.

Then comes the final sad scene. The spider approaches its helpless victim, bites it and starts sucking out all its blood and body-juices, growing fatter and fatter itself in the process till frequently it more than doubles its own size. The prey, on the other hand, collapses as an empty bag of outer skin or as an empty shell, should the victim happen to be a beetle. When all is over, the spider repairs the damage done to its web in the struggle; it does this at once, without postponing the work till some future opportunity. Then it returns to its position in the centre, pending the arrival of its next victim. Spiders are voracious and seem to possess an insatiable appetite.

This spider is very pugnacious and will fight to the death against any one of its own kind who attempts to tresspass into its web. I witnessed this for myself years ago, when I deliberately placed one of these spiders upon the web of a companion of the same species. A battle royal ensued, in the process of which legs were quickly torn off each combatant. The tresspaser lost in the end, after five of its legs had been bitten off by the spider who owned the web and who had lost two of its own legs in the battle. Those that remained, however, were enough to enmesh the trespasser securely in a ball of webbing. then came the *coup de grace,* the blood-sucking process, at which stage I ended my observations.

I brushed the web from my face and continued on our way. The *path* became narrower and the forest on both sides became dense. My torch-beam danced from one grey tree-trunk to the next; the moss and lichens that covered them looked like the beards of thousands of old men hanging to the ground.

Suddenly a stillness fell upon the jungle, a hush that could be felt as well as heard. Eric observed it, too, and quickened his steps. His toes kicked against my heels and he involuntarily touched my elbow. I halted in my tracks and he bumped into me. I extinguished the torch and sank down upon my haunches. In a jungle, the closer one can get to the ground, the better one can hear. For a moment Eric wondered where I was and groped with his hands in the darkness about me. Then he whispered 'Scotchie?'

It is a nickname by which I was known at school, though I rarely hear it today. My old schoolpals have practically disappeared. Many have gone abroad, while a large number have made the last journey we all must make. The thought makes me feel lonely at times.

I wondered what could be the cause of that hush, that almost palpable silence that hung so heavily about us. Reason told me there might be many explanations. The sudden cutting-off of the breeze that was blowing all this while from behind us by some hilly spur that we had circumvented in the darkness; an opposing breeze, blowing northwards up the great rift yawned before us in the night; a hush before a storm, a moment when all Nature appears to hold her breath in preparation for the fast approaching tempest.

The darkness was intense and there was no break in the gloom, even when I gazed upwards. the tree-tops were lost in obscurity and the stars that until a few moment ago were visible here and there through the canopy of leaves were now completely obliterated. That was when I came to know the reason for the strange silence that had fallen all around us. Indeed, a storm was approaching!

To witness such a phenomenon in the tropics is unforgettable, whether on land or at sea; but to have to undergo it upon the ground in a dense forest is hardly an enviable prospect. People sometimes run under a tree to shelter from the rain, but that is not the kind of rain we have in India, particularly in the jungles, and it certainly was no safe place when the tree itself might be split in two by lightning or torn up by the roots in the wind.

A moment later came a vivid flash overhead. It seemed to rend the canopy of the tree-tops and scatter the darkness with a single blaze of ethereal light. The heart of the storm was so close that it seemed but a fraction of a second before the thunderclap followed in an outrageous, monstrous roar, as of thousand cannon firing in unison. The earth upon which we stood shuddered and the overhanging foliage quivered with the resonance of the thunder; the very universe seemed to tremble.

There was nothing to do but crouch close to the ground. To remain standing is to invite injury from falling branches. Together we scrambled towards the trunk of a nearby tree. I made certain it was one of medium height and not one of the greater specimens whose top would reach to the upper trellises of the jungle, for the loftier the tree the more it would present itself as a target for the lightning which, in violent electrical storms of this kind, can be expected to strike at any moment.

The hush and the darkness returned, but not for long. There was another, more intense flash, followed by an even louder clap of thunder. The third flash was not a flash at all. Like a great serpent of fire from the sky, the lightning struck a giant tree somewhere in the jungle and the thunder that followed seemed to burst our eardrums and numb us with its intensity.

The next moment we heard a mighty, rushing uproar approaching towards us up the valley, like a hundred breakers in unison dashing upon a rocky beach. This was the wind and as it came closer one gained the impression that the trees of the forest were bracing themselves for the onslaught.

It was almost upon us now, and together with this fearsome, roaring sound we heard the staccato reports of hundreds of branches as they snapped like matchwood in the irresistible squall. Above the rushing of the wind we heard the louder thudding and crashing of falling branches and trees, and the creaking, tearing, and rending of timber. Here and there, trees of outstanding height or bulk, by reason of their top-weight and resistance to the wind, were uprooted from the earth and fell with resounding crashes, bringing down a host of minor trees and saplings that were unlucky enough to be sheltering below.

The gale continued for a few minutes only then passed as suddenly as it had begun. The trees lifted themselves again, many of them bereft of half their foliage. All was quiet for a short while except for the diminishing roar of the wind as it receded up the valley.

A new sound soon became audible, growing rapidly in intensity as it drew nearer: a continuous, hissing noise like escaping steam. The rain.

Now it was upon us. What was dry ground and foliage a moment earlier was in the twinkling of an eye converted into a sodden morass of mud and greenery. The best of umbrellas and raincoats would be of no avail in a downpour of this intensity, and we were carrying no umbrellas or raincoats anyway. Not only were we soaked to the skin, but the little equipment and food on our backs was equally saturated. Water poured down our bodies and flowed down our pants, filling our shoes, including my prized alpaca-lined boots, to the brim. This footwear was sold under a guarantee of being waterproof. It now proved the merit of that advertisement, but in an inverse manner. The water that had filled it remained where it was and refused to leak out.

The rain went on and on.

The little stream which was wont to purl and ripple over smooth, mossy stones as it meandered hither and thither, gliding down its course, did none of these nice things any longer. It dashed, lashed and smashed against the rocks in its course, accompanied by a thudding and grinding of torn branches and tree-trunks that were swept down by the flood. The water rose higher and covered the rocks and boulders that obstructed its *path*. it became a raging, unbroken flow, crested by the flotsam and jetsam that was whirled and tossed helplessly in the mad grip of the swirling flood.

The ground upon which we were standing was a foot deep in mud and there was not the slightest indication of the rain abating. But it lasted only a little more than an hour, and then it passed as swiftly as its precursor, the wind.

There were a million noises around us now, the dripping from the leaves, the gurgling rush of the stream, the frequent 'plop' from its banks as large section of earth, soaked by the rain and undermined by the raging torrent, collapsed into the flood.

We felt very miserable indeed. Unspoken thoughts turned to home, the comfort of bed and warm blankets, a steaming cup of tea, a relaxing pipe and a good book. What insane idea ever impelled us to start on a trip like this and place ourselves in such a predicament? Then recriminations passed. We forced ourselves to smile and begin to think what we should do next. We could only go back or press on. And who would think seriously of going back?

One thing was certain: we could not continue in our sodden clothing. As evaporation set in, our garments would grow colder and colder upon our bodies. Without clothes we could feel cold, admittedly, but at least we would not grow colder. However logical or illogical this argument might seem, we divested ourselves entirely, poured the water from our boots and put them on again. Our wet clothes we secured to pieces of bamboo, which we shouldered in addition to our kit.

Now we were ready to continue but far from comfortable, I can assure you. The bamboo dug itself into the flesh and the straps of our kitbags dug in too; thorns scraped our skins and our bare feet flopped about loosely in our boots; moreover, it was midnight and very cold.

Soon another hazard presented itself. We found ourselves slipping and slithering in the mud and ooze. The noise we were making by floundering along the soaked pathway and against the undergrowth on both sides of it would advertise our movements in the jungle for a furlong around. In any event, few animals would be on the move after the heavy downpour. Even the elephants would be inclined to call it a day—or rather, a night—and huddle together in some sheltered spot. Every creature would lie quiet; that is, every creature but the snakes! They would be up and about, hunting and gorging themselves upon the frogs that were making this night an occasion for rejoicing.

All around us we could hear these creatures croaking, particularly along the banks of the swollen stream. 'Korr! Korr! Korr! Quacker! Quacker! Quacker!' came the sound from a thousand bull-frog throats. The air droned with the noise. It vibrated and pulsated to the chorus of joy voiced by what was obviously the whole frog-population of the Spider Valley.

For this was mating time, and the forest floor was littered with squashy, lovemaking couples upon which we could not avoid treading in the darkness.

For a moment I caught a glimpse of something white in the middle of the *path*. Then it was gone. Again it appeared briefly and then disappeared once more. I could see the ground where it vanished and got the impression of movement, although I could not recognise what it was.

I came to a stop and directed the torch-beam steadily upon the movement. Eric halted behind me. For a few seconds I could not make out what lay on the pathway, then I knew what it was: a snake!

22

I increased my pace, motioning to Eric to remain where he was. Snakes have no ears, but they make up for lack of hearing by an acute sense of feeling. Through the scale upon their bellies that rest against the ground they are able to sense danger from anything that moves by detecting the vibration caused by that movement.

The boots I was wearing had soft rubber soles and I was able to approach relatively undetected. The beam of my torch was directed upon the reptile but it did not appear to be disturbed. Coming from behind, the source of the torchlight was beyond the range of the snake's vision. Snakes' eyes are lidless and fixed, and cannot turn sideways or backwards. Nor did my approach register itself upon the reptile's brain which, at the moment, was completely engrossed upon the work in hand, the swallowing of a very large bull-frog in one piece.

I was close enough now to make out the details. The snake's jaws, not being hinged together, were distended grotesquely and the gullet swollen out of all proportion. The head and one foreleg of the unfortunate frog had already disappeared down this passage, while the other three legs and the body hung limply outside. Normally, the creature should be kicking and struggling desperately to escape, but this frog was quite dead, and the reason was apparent. The snake was a cobra. The venom had killed the frog in a few seconds.

The cobra had not raised its hood in either alarm or anger, for it was still unaware of my approach, but the bulk of the bull-frog already in its gullet had sufficiently expanded the skin in the region to show up the characteristic V-mark. I was an ardent collector of snakes at that time, and the specimen before me was of outsize dimensions. I decided to catch it.

Unfortunately, the thick cloth bag I had brought for just such a purpose was with the kitbag on my back. I had to lay down the bamboo and my wet clothes before I could remove the kitbag from my back, and in all this movement the cobra became aware of our presence. It ejected the frog it had half-swallowed, turned around to face me and raised its hood, trembling with fury.

It was a magnificent specimen, but it would slither away in another second if I failed to put it into a fighting mood, so to do this I stamped my foot heavily upon the ground a couple of feet away. The cobra responded by raising itself still higher and then struck the ground at the spot where my foot had been but a moment before.

Meanwhile I was working feverishly to get the kitbag off my shoulders, unfasten the zip and grope with my hand amongst the many miscellaneous items in search of that snake-bag. The operation took a long time. The outside of the bag was soaking wet for one thing and I was working with one hand, unable to look for the bag as I had to keep my eyes fixed upon the cobra.

At last I found it, pulled it out quickly and advanced towards the snake, which turned itself fully around to face me.

Catching a cobra is really very easy once you rivet its attention. It is only when the reptile is in rapid motion that the operation becomes difficult and entails considerable risk. In this instance, I stretched out my right hand, holding the cloth bag by its handle close to the snake's head. It quivered with fury, hissed loudly, and lunged at the bag. That is when I withdrew the bag so that the cobra, with hood fully distended, struck its head upon the ground for the second time.

One has to be quick at this moment, but there is really nothing to it. The quickness of action comes with practice. The length of bamboo on which I had slung my wet clothes was in my left hand. It came in handy now. I quickly pressed down upon the snake's neck, behind its head and above the hood, with the end of this bamboo about six inches from its tip. The ground was wet, so I had to be careful not to allow the head to slip free. Eric was to be of no assistance to me. I saw that he had retired a good ten yards away. I called to him urgently to come and hold my torch. He advanced reluctantly and took it from me.

'Hold the light steady,' I admonished. Then I stooped down, dropped the cloth bag and grasped the snake behind its neck with the thumb and forefinger of my right hand. Then I removed the bamboo. The snake coiled itself around my hand and forearm, but I uncoiled it with my left hand while urging Eric to pick up the bag.

He hesitated and I repeated, 'Hurry up; pick it up and open it.'

It seemed to me as if Eric was taking a terribly long time to do just this, but eventually the bag was held in position and I forced the coils of the snake into it. Lastly I thrust the head inside, keeping the fingers of my left hand around the neck of the bag, released the snake's head and jerked my right hand out of the bag very quickly. Almost in one motion, I closed the neck of the bag with the fingers and thumb of my left hand.

That is all there is to catching a cobra. Some people have told me that it calls for nerve. Don't you believe that. In my opinion, it is just the opposite. There should be 'no nerve', or as few as possible. For if there are nerves, the snake-catcher may not be able to catch his snake. Worse still, he may hesitate in the middle of the operation, and that would be just too bad for him! The snake would catch him then with a bite upon his finger or hand.

I took care to tie up the neck of the bag very firmly and then thrust it back into my kitbag. A few minutes later we were on our way again.

For the next thirty minutes or so our discomfort Increased because of the wet and cold. It would have been nice to stop and light a fire to dry our clothing and ourselves, but the whole jungle was sodden and such an operation was out of the question. However we were young and ardently keen upon adventure. Mind conquers such obstacles and we pressed on forgetful of our physical discomfort. Except for encountering the elephants at the head of the valley, we had had no fun and we were longing for something to happen.

The stream began to flow rapidly now among steep rocks; the ground became hard and the trees and bamboos were shorter and more sparse. Larger expanses of sky were visible, and we noticed that the clouds had cleared. Myriads of stars hung over us and shone brightly.

The parallel ranges of mountains to the right and left of us, as we walked southwards, corresponded respectively to the western and eastern banks of the stream. Now we observed that they seemed to be converging upon each other while the valley narrowed to the proportions of a ravine. We could see the dark, unbroken outline of ridges and mountaintops on both sides as they towered upwards into the star-bedecked sky.

'Ayngh! Aa-u-ung! Oo-ooo ngh! Oo-ooo-ngh! Ooo-ooo-ooongh!'

We stopped in our tracks as we recognised that awesome sound. The canyon in which we were standing reverberated.

It was the call of the tiger! The animal was to our left and close ahead. It had come down the eastern range and was about to cross the stream. We extinguished our torches and hurried forwards to try to intercept it.

'Ugh! Ugh! Ugha!Ugha! Oooo-h! Ooo-h! Ooo-ooo-nigh! Aungh-ha! Ugh!Ugh'!

The call was almost continuous now. The tiger was being very noisy. Was this a sign of impatience? I seemed to detect an imperious note. Then remembered that this was the month of February. Rather late in February, admittedly, but nevertheless February still—the mating season or the tail end of it!

Here was the explanation of the prolonged semi-roars we were hearing. The beast was no tiger but a tigress. She was calling for a mate, and a tigress in this mood is not a very desirable creature to meet when unarmed.

As I have mentioned on many occasions, tigers are generally quite safe to meet, even when one is unarmed, with three exceptions—a man-eater, a wounded tiger, or a tiger in the mood for mating or in the act of mating. None of these conditions were literally fulfilled at that moment, but the third condition was very near.

The tigress continued her calling. She was but a short distance ahead now and still on our side of the stream. We were hurrying along that same bank. The stream was to our right. The flood water caused by the recent storm had abated considerably, but the stream must have been three or four feet deep at least. It the tigress intended to cross, she would have to swim.

As a rule tigers like water. Particularly in the hotter forests of Andhra Pradesh, I have come across them lying in shady pools to cool themselves when the temperature had reached over 110 degrees in the shade. But it was rather doubtful if this tigress would trust herself to cross the stream which was still foaming and frothing with the extra water fed to it from a myriad trickles reaching it from the forest on both sides.

At that moment my conjectures were interrupted by a fresh sound: 'Wrr-ung!Ar-ung! Arr-ungh! Oo-ooon!'

It was louder by far than the noise made by the tigress and the roar of water besides.

A tiger! He had heard and answered the call of a mate. The tigress heard it too. She answered with a loud 'Ugh! Ahha-ha-ha-ha!' of delight.

27

We were still in darkness. To flash our torches now would make our presence known. Most probably both tigers would disappear, unless they actively resented our company. Things would not be so pleasant then. But if we remained in darkness our presence would probably not be detected, as tigers have no sense of smell, while the noise of the stream would muffle any noise we might inadvertently make.

Our eyes had accustomed themselves to the starlight as we came to a halt and stood behind a tree that bordered the track. A few feet to our right was the bank of the stream. Beyond that and to our left, the jungle was a wall of darkness lit by a thousand flickering, moving lights, the fireflies that dart to and fro in ceaseless motion. The tumbling waters reflected countless stars, and here and there we could make out the darker forms of bushes or clumps of coarse grass on the bank. Of movement of any kind, we could see nothing.

Both tigers had now stopped calling. For them to meet, one or the other would have to ford the stream that lay between. The question was, which would be the one to cross? If the tigress crossed, we would be safe. If the tiger came over, both animals would be very close to us and would certainly resent our presence if they detected us.

The tigress clinched the matter by calling once more. This time she was almost mewing, like a very gruff and hoarse cat. Like all females in her circumstances, she was revelling in her position of advantage and was enticing the male to come to her; she would not condescend to go to him. Would the tiger be able to resist such a temptation?

He roared and roared again. It was a roar of defiance and challenge at the same time. Clearly he was warning all other tigers to keep away from his newly-founded mate. The tigress, still on our bank, continued her enticing mewing.

As I expected, the tiger could resist no longer. A long, dark silhouette emerged from the black wall of forest on the other bank, hesitated for a few seconds and then slid into the water of the stream.

I have already said that this watercourse is neither broad nor deep and it took him a very short time to cross. The silhouette became a solid grey form as he waded and then walked ashore, perhaps some fifty yards away.

All this while the tigress had not revealed herself. She now broke cover with a bound, herself another grey shape, leaped forward to meet the tiger with a loud growl and reared up on her hind legs to slap him across his neck. The mock-fighting in which mating tigers indulge was about to begin. Neither animal intends to hurt the other, but frequently during this fighting, through excitement or a stray bite or scratch, tempers run high and the tigress invariably gets really rough. The tiger tolerates a lot until she at last goes too far. Then he loses his temper and sets about her in real earnest.

Both animals can be badly scratched and bitten and bleed freely by the time the repeated mating is over, but both animals appear to revel in the routine, soon forget their differences and cling together as a couple till the cubs are about to be born, at which time the tigress will separate herself from her lord for a while through fear that he might devour the cubs. Thereafter they will rejoin for maybe a year, along with their cubs, when they will part to seek fresh mates with the next season, approximately two years after the last, although the cubs sometimes remain with their mother for a few months more.

We had lost our chance of beating a retreat while the going was good before the tiger crossed the stream. Now that he was only a few yards away, and moreover because the tigress was with him, the slightest movement on our part would betray our presence to one or both the animals. If that should happen, our extinction was more than probable as both the felines, and particularly the male would not tolerate our eavesdropping on their lovemaking. It is equally likely that the tigress, in the excitement of mating, would resent our presence. It was too late now, anyway, to do anything about it. The only course open to us was to sink down to earth behind the tree-trunk that hid us and hope that the mating animals would not move in our direction.

For the next hour we were compelled to listen to a pandemonium of grunts, snarls, roars, prolonged mewing and a medley of other noises as the two animals pursued their lovemaking, the sounds differing in accordance with their mood and temper at each moment. As the mating progressed to reach climax, the loveplay became rougher and rougher, until it reached a point when they were almost fighting each other tooth and nail. In mating the tiger bites the female in the neck and literally holds her down. They then separate a while and rest before starting all over again.

Several times, in the course of their gambols and struggles, they dashed hither and thither, on more than one occasion coming within ten yards of us. Occasionally, we thought we were discovered and prepared to make a dash for it, although we knew such a step would only hasten our destruction. The tree that hid us was too thick to climb, and the next was twenty feet away, but we could not climb it together. The first to reach it might possibly escape, provided the tigers did not follow him up, but the second man would be doomed. So we stayed where we were.

Finally the two felines tired of their efforts. The tigress curled up to rest like a cat, while the tiger sat on his haunches beside her to recuperate. And we wondered if they would never go away.

The placid scene was broken by a roar from the further bank. Another tiger, a male, had heard the sounds of revel and had come to see if there was chance to join in. The first tiger at once sprang to his feet to give an answering roar in challenge to the newcomer. The tigress uncurled herself, stood on her four legs twitched her tail from side to side, and then settled down on her haunches. Clearly she was enjoying the situation, no doubt extremely pleased with herself at the prospect of two males about to engage in a titanic contest on her account.

The tiger on the further bank answered the challenge with roars of his own. Then he broke cover and stood revealed. Now the two males faced each other, the stream between them. The tigress, upon her haunches still, snarled mildly, mewed and almost purred in glee. It was obvious she was enjoying herself. This provoked the first tiger beyond endurance. Coughing a loud 'Whoff! Whoff! Whoff!,' he entered the stream and rushed at his rival. The level of the water appeared to have dropped appreciably, for this time he was able to wade the whole distance.

The challenger awaited his coming, coughing and roaring. The first tiger reached the other bank, crouched low for a moment, and then hurled himself at his rival.

But something quite unexpected happened at the last moment. All this while the newcomer had given every indication that he was prepared to stand and do battle for the handsome female across the stream, but as her first lover crouched for his final spring, his courage turned to water. He whirled around and bolted for dear life. Seeing this and gathering momentum the first tiger charged after him with a series of victorious roars.

The female on our bank, disappointed that there was not going to be a fight for her favours, but anxious now to endear

31

herself to her lord, coughed once and galloped across the stream to follow the two males that had vanished into the blackness of the jungle.

At that Eric and I lost no time. We raced away to get out of the vicinity of the three tigers and leave them to settle their lovemaking problems. We stumbled along through the gloom for the best part of half a mile before we risked switching on our torches again, for we did not dare to attract the attention of the three animals who had gone up the rising ground across the stream and might return at any moment.

From the contours of the surrounding mountains as silhouetted against the sky, I knew we were approaching the hamlet of Kempekerai. It was here that I shot the tiger I called the 'Novice of Manchi'. At this point the pathway we were following crossed the stream and we waded through the water which now reached just above our knees. The track leads up a slope to the hamlet, and we followed it till we reached the mud-wattle huts of Kempekerai.

A cur barked but none of the inmates bothered to stir, and it was only after repeated calling that a very tousled and sleepy head was thrust from a slightly-opened doorway. The half-closed eyes blinked in the glare of my torch. The head and eyes were those of my old friend Byra the poojaree, of whom I have told you in other stories. For the greater part of the year this man lived with his wife and children almost stark naked in a burrow called 'gavvies' excavated in the steep banks of the Chinar river. When the rains came and the Chinar rose and the earth of the 'gavvies' turned too soft and was liable to collapse and close the burrow in which they lived, the whole family took service as cattle-grazers under some rich agriculturist, who sent his herd of cattle into the reserved forests to graze upon the long grass that spring up after the rains.

The agriculturist had to pay in licence to the government for grazing his cattle. In those days this fee was four *annas* (a fraction below four pence) per head for the whole period of five months grazing. The usual procedure was to buy a licence for about fifty head of cattle, paying the government twelve-and-a-half rupees as grazing fee (at the rate of sixteen *annas* to the rupee), but to drive anything up to 200 head— or even more—into the forest. A small gratuity of five rupees to the forest guard would cover the grazing fee for the remaining 150 unlicensed animals.

To look after these 200 beasts, Byra and his family would have to build what was called a *patti*, which was nothing more than a small clearing in the jungle. A smaller circular fence of thorns was constructed within this clearing for actually sheltering the cattle from wild animals at night. It was in the style of the African 'boma', with the difference that, as there are no lions in south India, the thorn fence would not be more than a yard in height and not very thick either. Tigers and panthers are not given to vaulting over thorn fences and carrying off their prey, as are the more daring lions of Africa that hunt in groups.

The hamlet of Kempekerai was nothing more than a multiple cattle *patti*, accommodating not only Byra and his family but a number of other families as well, all of them engaged in looking after different herds of cattle belonging to different owners. As a result, the animals actually in residence at any of these multiple *pattis* exceeded, by at least five times, the stipulated number of cattle permitted to graze in that area under licence from the forest department; the government got less than one-fifth of the revenue in cattle-licences that it should have collected; the forest guard received an amount in bribes at least equal to, if not more than, his official salary; the owners of the herds had made a good arrangement; the grass, shrubs and the saplings of certain varieties of succulent trees were eaten down and destroyed over a large area of forest; the deer suffered by losing that amount of grazing; 'foot-and-mouth' disease, rife among village cattle, spread and decimated the deer, bison and wild boar in the jungle; and everybody was happy, including the tigers and panthers in the area, who with easier hunting got a good deal more to eat, preying upon the domestic herds. Happiest of all were the jackals, hyaenas and vultures that ate the cattle that died, whether by disease or by being killed by other wild animals.

This is indeed a true picture of the state of affairs in those good old days till a certain deadly poison was introduced as an insecticide by the government and made available to farmers, almost free of charge, to protect the crops from insect pests.

Some peasant then discovered that the insecticide, intended to kill caterpillars, beetles and other such pests, would also kill tigers and panthers that preyed upon the domestic herds and, far more important, unwanted mothers-in-law, brother-in-law, in fact all 'in-laws' of both sexes and all ages with happy impartiality, not to mention secret lovers, rivals, elder brothers who were so inconsiderate as to inherit the property when father died, and a whole host of other unwanted characters into the bargain. To put it in a nutshell, opportunity was rife for those who were disgruntled in one way or another.

The carcasses of cattle killed by tigers and panthers were systematically doctored with the result that the felines died in hundreds and have been almost wiped out in southern India. Along with them jackals, hyaenas and vultures, who shared these kills, perished in still larger numbers. There was also a sharp rise in the number of in-laws and other inconvenient people who began to succumb, suddenly, mysteriously and in increasing numbers, to violent stomachache and other alarming symptoms. Life is cheap and nobody worried unduly, while the statisticians were compensated slightly in the other graph they were maintaining with regard to the vexatious problem of 'Population Explosion and Family Planning' which happened to coincide with the advent of the poison.

To this day, unlicensed still exceed the licensed cattle by many times. The owners save that much money in license fees, the forest guards draw more than their salary now, the government loses much more, and everyone is still happy. The only difference from the old days is that there are now no tigers, panthers, hyaenas, jackals or even vultures to join in the general rejoicing. Nearly all are dead—poisoned.

Incidentally, the villagers were not taking very kindly to the family-planning programmes. In fact, the greater number of them were distinctly annoyed about the whole thing. On the one hand, they were being urged to mechanise their farming methods and give up the old-fashioned, cattle-drawn wooden ploughs of their forefathers. At the same time, the cost of living and the prices of all commodities were rising day by day. The monsoon had a knack of not arriving when it should and of coming when it should not. Either way their crops failed. Landlords were more grasping and so were the moneylenders. The government had tried to help all it could by distributing land, oxen and ploughs free of cost to any family in order to assist farmers who preferred to stick to the old style; but money, that root of all evil, was a temptation, and the oxen and ploughs were sold or mortgaged shortly after they were distributed. The land would have followed suit as well, but that was rather too great a risk to take, being immovable property.

Finally, the price of kerosene was increasing by leaps and bounds. One could not afford to burn the midnight oil. An early dinner and early to bed became the golden rule.

In the midst of all these troubles, the poor ryot had but one consolation left to him—his cherished and beloved wife. At least she belonged to him, to do with as he wanted. What with rising costs, no kerosenre, an early dinner and early to bed, he had at least some opportunity here. She was the one solid item that was entirely his own. But at this stage along came these Family Planning people with their ridiculous advice, offering strange devices their forefathers had never heard of and begrudging the poor farmer the one and only pleasure and recreation available to him in these hard days.

So the statisticians were worried at the still steadily rising curve of population, although a trifle relieved that here and there would appear a slight kink in it, caused by the untimely demise of some in-laws and others who had succumbed to a sudden unaccountable and unbearable stomach pain that had come on immediately after dinner.

All of which brings us back to Byra the poojaree, my old friend of the jungle. Byra was very happy when he discovered that the visitor arriving at such an unearthly hour was none other than myself. He crawled out of the narrow doorway of his hut and offered the accustomed greeting of the poojarees by touching his forehead to the ground before me. Then we sat down for a chat and I told him the reason for our presence.

The jungle man was surprised and not a little concerned at the fact that we were unarmed. He thought that we were taking too great a risk, especially with elephants, and gave us the disconcerting news that there was a particularly 'bad' elephant roaming that part of the valley we had yet to negotiate. Whereas this elephant had not yet been proclaimed a 'rogue', inasmuch as it had not actually killed anybody; it was an animal that charged on sight and only the fleetness of foot and jungle-cunning of the poojarees of Kempekerai had saved them, at least so far. Byra doubted that we had that fleetness or cunning and advised us not to continue our journey that night.

'Wait for daylight,' he advised. 'At least, then you will be able to see where you are running when he chases you, although I doubt that will do you much good.'

The other reason why Byra was annoyed by the fact that we were not carrying firearms was his hope that he might have persuaded one or other of us to shoot a sambar or spotted deer for his family and himself to eat. This was Byra's only weakness, his craving for meat. Every time we met it was the same thing. He would pester me to shoot a deer or sambar, and just as steadfastly I refused. Money I was ready to give him, but I had explained a hundred times that I do not like killing deer and sambar. Although he has never succeeded in his efforts to break me down on this point, Byra never fails to try and try again. Possibly he thinks that he will wear me down eventually, and so must have our preliminary struggle every time we meet.

Eric and I decided to eat and bring out our sandwiches. Unfortunately they contained beef, an ingredient that is forbidden to nearly all south Indians, including the humblest forest folk. The cow is sacred, and to eat its flesh is outrageously and unthinkably sinful. So although we did not make the mistake of offering him any, there was a distinct look of disapproval on Byra's simple face. Eating beef was one of two things that he held against me; of the other I have just spoken. On all other matters he felt we were buddies or, to use a slang expression, 'as thick as thieves'.

Considering he had never been to school, this man, aborigine as he was, was an authority on jungle medicines obtained from flowers, fruits, leaves, roots and barks of various trees and herbs. He was the 'doctor' of the surrounding poojaree community and had been summoned in emergencies to cure all sorts of illnesses. He had a secret remedy for snake-bite, and had not lost a single case, or so he said. I know for a fact he cured two cases of cholera when that dreaded epidemic spread to his community, and, as I have mentioned in one of my books, he delivered his own wife when she was having her baby.

I have witnessed this and his method was very simple. He prepared a shallow hollow in the sands of the nearest stream, and into this hollow he put a thick layer of green leaves. In this hollow his wife lay down on her back. Next he got a torn piece of saree cloth and tied one end to the soles of her feet. This cloth was only long enough to reach to her.knees. Byra gave this end to hold with both hands, and to do so the woman had to part her thighs and knees, which she raised off the ground. Byra then instructed her to pull hard upon the end, whereupon, with hardly a whisper, the baby was born and Byra welcomed it into this world by raising it by the heels and slapping it on the back. He had no scissors, so the sharp end of a stone or mussel-shell (which could be found along the banks of most steams), operating against a flat stone, served to sever the cord.

Within half an hour of the appearance of the placenta, the wife rose, suckled her infant and walked away. Byra then shovelled the sand into the hollow until it was entirely filled.

Knowing my weakness for tea Byra had already made a fire, and on this I placed my canteen filled with water from the stream. It was very muddy and the resultant brew was rather substandard. I told the poojaree of our encounter with the three tigers not far upstream, and he said that these three were the only ones in residence there at that moment. There had been another female, but she had wandered away some months earlier and had not returned. He went on to say that frequently one or other of the three tigers would attack the herds while the cattle were grazing in the forest and kill one of the cows.

The tigress had been calling quite a lot recently, he confirmed. The poojarees in the hamlet had heard her only two nights earlier. All three animals were cattle-lifters, but none of them had shown any inclination to attack the graziers, who had frequently driven them away from their kills to salvage the hides for drying and sale. He added that there was also a pair of panthers living on the other side of the stream that occasionally killed a stray cow if opportunity allowed. A month earlier, one of these panthers had pulled down a calf and was killing it when one of the tigers rushed out of the undergrowth, put the panther to flight and carried the calf away, slung across its back.

We stood up to leave, when Byra once again remonstrated about the great risk we were running with the 'bad' elephant. However, to remain in shelter at the *patti* for the rest of the night was not jungle 'ghooming', and ghooming was the purpose of the trip. We explained this to the poojaree and shouldered our loads, but not before I checked to make certain that the cobra was still safely secured.

'Very well then; I will go with you', the little man announced. 'When the sun rises I will return. Till then, I shall remain with you and offer what protection lies in my power. I don't think you realise the danger you will be in if you happen to meet the elephant in this darkness', he stressed, 'for the beast will be upon you before you know where you are and crush you to a pulp.'

With these ominous words in our ears we left Kempekerai and headed downhill to the stream. I led, shining the torch; Byra followed me, while Eric brought up the rear. We reached and crossed the water and followed the narrow *path* before us into the labyrinths of the jungle. It was distinctly chilly and a junglecock, crowing among the bamboos, reminded us it was two in the morning. Like their cousins, the domestic roosters, wild cocks follow the same habits in the jungles that are not unduly disturbed by men or too many wild cats. They crow at two and at four in the morning, and just after the false dawn, usually before six o'clock.

We might have covered a half-mile when Byra stepped up from behind and halted me with his hand upon my arm. He reached forward to extinguish the torch. Eric half-asleep now collided with us before he realised we had stopped. I strained my ears, but heard no sound. The junglecock had passed out of hearing range.

The stars cast a sheen over the forest that was quite different from moonlight. It was a soft and ethereal light that just succeeded in making itself felt in the darkness without breaking its dominion. The forest that surrounded us was as black as a bottomless pit, the starlight being enough only to see each other and the few yards around us.

I looked at Byra inquiringly. He touched his nose with the forefinger and thumb of his left hand, at the same time swinging his right arm, from elbow downwards, to right and left before him.

The elephant! Byra could smell it! It must be very close indeed, or the poojaree would have whispered his message in my ear.

I wrinkled my nose in an effort to catch the scent. At the same time I turned my head sideways, one cheek in the direction we were moving and the other in the direction whence we had come. I fancied I could detect a peculiar odour which within a few seconds I began to associate with the presence of an elephant. These animals smell strongly when they are close. But perhaps it was a figment of my imagination.

My cheeks told me there was hardly a breeze blowing from any direction, a fact that was neither good nor bad. Had the breeze been blowing from behind us, the elephant—provided there was one ahead—would have scented us by now. Had the breeze been blowing from him to us, we might have been able, exercising the greatest caution, to creep past him undetected. As matters stood, with practically no breeze in any direction, our situation was one of stalemate. The elephant—supposing there was one ahead—had not so far detected our presence. But he was bound to do so if we moved any closer. Even if he did not scent us, he would certainly hear us in that deathly silence.

Byra had come to the same conclusion much earlier. He raised his right palm at waist level. The signal was plain as if he had spoken: 'Wait!' Tensely we stood quite motionless.

The moments dragged by. We heard no sound. I could smell the strange odour still, but I could not associate it with an elephant. Perhaps Byra was wrong after all and there was no elephant before us.

Then the silence was broken. We heard a rustling sound, growing louder and heavier and moving along the pathway on which we were standing. Byra had been right. There was an elephant ahead, and he was moving through the undergrowth in our direction. It was only a matter of seconds before he would emerge upon the pathway.

Byra signalled to us to retreat and gave the lead by turning around and walking on tiptoe down the track along which we had just come. Eric followed, and I brought up the rear.

At that moment the breeze decided to take a hand. A gust blew strongly down the valley, passing over us and directly towards the elephant. The cat was now out of the bag!

The elephant scented us and in the next instant was crashing through the rest of the undergrowth. He came out upon the track behind me. Still retreating, all three of us turned around. We could see his colossal black bulk now, like a great big black rock astride the track. Two long streaks of white stood out against that blackness. His tusks!

A moment later and we knew, indeed, that this was the 'bad' elephant about which Byra had warned us. For no sooner did the beast set eyes upon us than he recognised us for his avowed enemies—men. He trumpeted his shriek of hate and came charging towards us, looking blacker and bigger at every instant.

To run away would be hopeless. At so short a distance no man can escape a charging elephant. Either Eric or myself, encumbered as we both were with our loads, would fall a prey to this monster. He would smash to a jelly whichever one of us he caught first. To try to dodge into the bushes either to right or left was equally hopeless because of the darkness. It looked as if only Byra would live to tell the tale.

I did the only thing possible in the circumstances. I took a very flimsy chance. I stopped, turned around. At the same time I yelled with all my might.

The bright beam fell fully upon the monster, scarcely ten feet away. In a peculiarly detached and interested fashion, I noticed that the animal had curled in his trunk, that his head was raised, showing a half-opened mouth, and that the points of his tusks were in line with his small, gleaming, wicked eyes. He lowered his head to bring those tusks into line with me and thus let the torchlight fully into his eyes. The next instant a cloud of dust hid the ground and the elephant's legs.

I was still screaming when I realised that the brute had come to a halt. Braking suddenly, by planting his four great feet in the ground, was the cause of the dust.

I did not know it then, but seeing the peril I was in made Byra stop, turn around and come to my assistance. He was screaming too, I suddenly realised; words of ludicrous, vile abuse to the elephant, all of its kind and its ancestors. Eric had dashed past him and was still in full flight. He did not mean to desert me but had not realised that the elephant was so close as to compel me to turn around and face him.

The next few moments were electric. What was going to happen next was a matter of life or death. Would the pachyderm press his attack home, or would Byra and I succeed in turning him?

With sinking heart I remembered Byra's words of warning, uttered but a short while earlier. Once it charged, nothing would stop this elephant.

The monster shook his head from right to left and back again several times, with the purpose of avoiding the piercing beam of my torch that shone fully into his eyes. But I followed his movements with my torch, still shouting lustily.

The brute stood his ground. Then I took the last chance left. Yelling like a maniac, I stepped forward sharply, directing the beam fully into those small, wicked eyes. Then his courage broke. he turned half around so that his huge bulk, facing broadside on, straddled the narrow track.

Without speaking to each other, Byra and I knew that it was now or never. With concerted shouts, we rushed towards the monster, my torch still shining directly upon its head. The elephant was unnerved. Like all big bullies, he was accustomed to attack and see his enemies scatter like chaff before the wind. Never before had any puny creature dared to attack him.

That was exactly what was happening now. He could not get that glaring light out of his eyes and our discordant screams were unnerving him. So he lumbered up the pathway away from us, Byra and I behind him, still shouting at the top of our voices. To shake us off, he swerved sharply to the left and crashed through the undergrowth.

Byra and I came to a stop. We had accomplished his rout. Now we had to get away as quickly as possible. Turning once again we walked back the way we had come. It would not do for us to run, for that might bring the elephant back. We could find no traces of Eric!

It was but half-a-mile to the spot where we had to cross the stream to return to Kempekerai, but Eric did not know the place. Probably he had passed it and continued along the track beyond.

Byra broke into a trot to try overtake him, while I walked rapidly on. I was not feeling so good. In fact, I was feeling awfully sick and I noticed that I was shaking as if in fever and did not seem to be able to stop. Also I was soaking wet—perspiration no doubt, although I did not remember perspiring so much. I toyed with the idea of sitting down for a few moments but the thought came to me that the black devil might change its mind and return to the attack. So I walked all the faster. Very soon I reached the ford leading to Kempekerai, and there was no sign of Eric or Byra.

I splashed through the stream and climbed the winding *path* to the hamlet. Reaching the huts I threw myself on the ground to get rid of the nausea that had not yet passed away.

It was some time before Byra arrived with Eric. The poojaree told me that my friend was a good runner. He had to follow for almost two miles before he succeeded in overtaking Eric. Eric's version was that when he glanced back, but could see neither Byra nor myself, he concluded that the elephant had got both of us. This had made him run all the faster.

Byra seemed quite unperturbed by our recent adventure. To him it was part of everyday forest existence. He suggested we brew some tea. If there was one thing Byra had a weakness for, it was tea. So have I, but for once I did not feel up to drinking any. Throwing down my haversack, I told him and Eric to help themselves. Then I lay down on the bare earth and fell asleep.

The sun was shining brightly when I awoke. Eric was sleeping soundly close by, lying neatly on his groundsheet, covered with a light blanket. Byra was coiled almost into a ball by the side of a small fire that had long gone out. His head was touching his knees.

My teeth were chattering with the cold. Lying on the ground with no covering had made matters worse. In the chill of the morning, when enthusiasm is usually at an ebb, I wondered if the risks we had taken the previous night were justified. I remembered reading in an article somewhere or the other, that it is at such a time—when one first awakens— that the influence of the subconscious mind is at its strongest, and the impressions one receives at the moment conveyed the wisest and best advice. It went on to say that, should the recipient follow this advice, he would prosper and avoid the pitfalls of living. But these few moments of good sense pass all too swiftly, the article continued, to give place to the individual's own individuality and way of thinking, and he then relapses into his own fixed ideas.

I fear this is what happened to me, for those minutes of common sense were put aside. I aroused Eric and Byra, and while the latter relit the fire to brew our tea, Eric and I went down to the stream for a cold bath and brush-up. It is wonderful what a bath in a mountain stream will do for the cobwebs in one's brain, and for muscles that ache and eyes that are still heavy from insufficient sleep.

By the time we returned, Byra had not only boiled the water and made the tea, but had drunk more than half of it himself. He offered a ready excuse for this by saying that he felt the fever coming on, and as the *dorai* knew very well, plenty of tea is the only prescription for averting fever. I replied that the dorai had never known this but would bear it in mind by dishing out less of the ingredients that go to make the beverage the next time. Then Eric and I finished what was left.

A cold breakfast, followed by a smoke and some desultory chat, led Byra to ask what we intended doing next. I replied that we would sleep for most of that day and start again with nightfall to finish our journey at the point where the stream joins the Chinar river. This we expected to reach about midnight. After another short rest, we would start to return, accomplishing the trip this time by daylight. We hoped to get to Aiyur by dusk the following evening, when 'Sudden Death' ought to get us back to Bangalore in time for dinner.

The poojaree was not happy to learn our plans. He implied, by indirect comparison with a donkey which, in spite of being repeatedly beaten yet refuses to go forward, that we had failed to learn our lesson at the hands of the elephant, by wanting to pass through his domain once again after darkness. He suggested we start about two in the afternoon instead, when all pachyderms take, or should take, their siestas by standing asleep in the shelter of some thick clump of tress, so that by nightfall we should be well away from the places where *pisachee* (devil) usually hung out. Of course, if our luck was bad, he might have gone further afield, in which case we might still run into him, but at least that risk was not as great as would be the case by starting after dark. Byra also insisted upon accompanying us as far as the Chinar river and back again, saying he would not leave us till we were at least five miles on the return journey between Kempekrai and Aiyur, where we had left the car.

We discussed the matter and wiser, if less adventurous, counsel prevailed. We decided to follow Byra's plan and, as there was nothing better to do, we fell asleep. Soon after midday we ate a cold lunch, followed by more tea, and at exactly two o'clock were on our way again, retracing our steps on the narrow pathway along which we had so precipitously bolted the night before. But this time we could look about us and take all possible precautions by testing the wind and keeping a sharp lookout for signs of the elephant.

We were unlucky from the start. A strong wind was blowing from north to south, that is, down the stream from behind us and in the direction we were going. It would inform the rogue of our approach should he be anywhere ahead.

Plainly, on the damp earth of the narrow pathway, we could see our own footmarks: the blurred impressions of Eric's rubber shoes, the larger marks made by my own alpaca-lined boots, Byra's bare footsteps, and imposed upon them all the ponderous, almost dish-sized tracks left by the elephant that had chased us the night before.

Byra was in front. Every now and then he stopped to test the wind by plucking a few blades of grass from the ground and dropping them from shoulder-height. Imperceptibly, they fell to earth at a slight angle ahead of us. The wind was still blowing from behind.

Byra stopped to listen. We halted and listened too. The forest was athrob with life. Birds twittered all round. We could hear their more distant calls from the hillsides to right and left. Cicadas and crickets of all varieties chirped in different cadences. The single, shrill resonance of the plains-cicada is here mixed with the rising and falling sonority of the hill variety, smaller in size than its cousin of lower-lying areas but capable of emitting a far louder sound. Then a myriad crickets of all sizes, ensconced beneath leaves or hidden under rotting logs of wood, joined in the general vibration of insect vociferation, filling the air with the sound of throbbing, omnipresent life.

Far ahead of us a barking-deer learned of our approach. The wind blowing down the valley told him. 'Kharr!' he cried, and again and again 'Kharr! Kharr!'

The langur monkeys, high up on both hillsides, heard him. 'Whoomp! Whoomp! Whoomp!' they shouted in sheer glee, leaping from branch to branch and rock to rock. But the little barking-deer continued his alarm-cry.

This worried the langurs. Their whoomps of joy died down. Now they were silent. I could picture the langur-watchman, seated on tree-top, peering hard into the valley below, trying to discover the nature of the danger that had alarmed the little deer. The shaggy brows in his round black face must be beetled with worry and uncertainty; his large, round, black eyes must be searching the streambed far below and such game-paths as were visible to him from that height, in an effort to see the foe. He was responsible for the safety and lives of the numerous she-monkeys and babies of the tribe gambolling in innocence around him. Should he fail in his duty, by failing to give the alarm, one of them would die. No doubt he thought that at any moment he would see the stripes of a tiger or the spotted coat of a panther slinking from bush to bush.

He saw nothing, for we were yet too far away.

Nevertheless the little deer, whose keen sense of smell had told him of something the langur could not see, announced our approach by continuing to bark and bark, 'Kharr! Kharr! Kharr!'

The langur-watchman became increasingly uneasy. What kind of foe was this, approaching but invisible?

At last he could stand the tension of uncertainty no longer. He had to warn the tribe. 'Harr! Ha!' he shouted gutturally, and again in quick succession, 'Harr! Ha! Harr! Ha!'

The alarm had its effect at once. Although we could not see or hear them, there followed a hundred thuds as langur-mothers clutched their babies to their breasts and leapt prodigious distances to safety in the loftiest tree-tops. Others scampered up rocks or ran up the hillside. A hundred black faces turned in anxiety to their watchman. What enemy had he seen? His next action would tell them.

If a tiger or panther were approaching, the watchman would, surely leap from his tree-top to another. He would stand on his two feet, with long tail erect to keep his balance, look downwards and abuse the enemy in langur-language.

The watchman did none of these things. He still had not seen us. So he continued his alarm, 'Harr! Ha!' and again 'Harr! Ha!' A sambar stag, resting on a bed of high grasses somewhere up the mountainside to our left, heard the commotion. He sprang to his feet and cried 'Dhank! Dhank! Honk!' These signals of alarm from the different denizens of the forest had not sounded in vain. They were heard by listening and understanding ears. Ponderous ears, indeed. For at that precise moment the elephant struck again.

Decades old, and wise in the ways of the jungle, he had been hearkening and hiding in motionless silence. He had heard the alarm-cry of the barking-deer, the calls of the langur-watchman and the belling of the disturbed sambar stag. Undoubtedly he had smelt us, too, for he was standing much nearer and knew that it was the hated human foe who had come again.

He made up his mind quickly. This time he was not going to fail in his purpose. His purpose was to destroy one of the hated, two-legged foes. He would wait in silence till we walked right up to him. Then and then only would he charge. By this means he was sure to catch one of us.

We knew nothing of his presence or what was passing in his evil mind. Despite his size, he remained hidden by a rock to our left behind which he had taken up his position. For once Byra, man of the forests as he was and versed in jungle-lore from childhood, and with unnumbered generations of jungle-ancestors before him, was deceived. Walking warily in the lead, with Eric and myself following light-footed behind, he moved forward step by step.

Byra saw the big rock to his left and halted to study it carefully. We saw it, too, and stopped to look. It was a large, high, loaf-shaped rock, almost black in colour except for two large patches of grey lichen growing upon its surface. A fig tree clung to one side of it. We noticed that some of the roots of this tree had run over the rock. One root strayed down the side, resembling a long, thick, light-coloured snake going into the ground.

All this we saw. But we did not see the elephant hiding behind that rock, because he made neither sound nor movement.

Byra was satisfied that there was no danger and that it was safe to proceed. He walked forwards slowly. We followed.

Now we stood abreast to the rock. Now we began to pass it. The elephant knew then that in another second we would see him. He also knew that now we were so close that he must be able to catch at least one of us. He made up his mind.

An ear-splitting scream rent the silence: 'Tri-aa-aa-ank!' Then he was upon us. He meant business this time for he did not utter another sound. From behind the rock his black form emerged. The great trunk was coiled inwards like a giant snake, behind high-thrown head and flattened ear. His mouth was half-open.

Eric, in front of me, turned and ran. So did I. Instinctively, Byra knew that if he followed he would be caught, as he would be a third man running behind two others, who would baulk him. He decided to swerve and try to escape by running downhill and across the stream which flowed parallel to the pathway we were following.

He had no chance. The elephant was upon him. It uttered a short and muffled half-scream, above which I heard Byra's shriek of despair. There was 'whoosh' followed by a thud. The elephant then gave vent to his rage by trumpeting repeatedly: 'Tri-aaa-ank! Tri-aaa-ank! Tri-aa-ank!'

I was running as fast as my clumsy boots would let me. Eric younger in years, lighter in build, and wearing soft shoes, overtook me and disappeared ahead. I am ashamed to say that I continued to run. I know I should have stopped and gone to Byra's aid. Of small consolation was the thought that unarmed as I was, there was nothing I could do, and as the elephant was thoroughly enraged my shouts would not deter him. The night before, my torch beam in the darkness had confused him. Now he would finish me off as well.

The elephant had stopped. I could hear him screaming still. He was probably trampling poor Byra to pulp.

I reached the crossing. Eric was on the other side of the stream. A short distance higher lay Kempekerai and safety. As hurriedly as possible we recruited all the poojarees in the hamlet. Torches of wood and grasses were made. Embers to light them were carried in broken pots. Two dozen in number, we recrossed the stream, set the torches alight, and with the whole party shouting at the top of their voices, we set forth to gather what remained of my poor friend.

The elephant was silent, although we expected him to show at any moment. Would he charge our party?

I did not think so. We were two dozen strong and we were making a terrific noise.

The next moment we saw him. He was standing squarely upon the pathway. Irritably, he was shaking his head from side to side, his great trunk wagging along with the motion. His ears were flapping forwards. We could see his bloodshot little eyes staring at us. Clearly he was undecided as to whether to charge or beat a retreat.

Each member of our party excelled himself that day. Every one was shouting louder still, if that were possible. The elephant continued to hesitate. Then his nerve failed. He turned about; then he faced around again. Unexpectedly, he made off up the hill to our left. We advanced cautiously, continuing to yell.

At each moment we expected to come across the remains of the luckless Byra, squashed to a pulp. I could picture the little man before me, his grin spreading from ear to ear, and two jet-black little eyes gleaming with laughter. The vision choked me. I could join in the shouting no longer. The little man had sacrificed his life to save us. Had he escaped, the elephant would have followed and got one of us. Eric, walking beside me, looked grim, although he continued to yell with the rest.

But we could not find the remains of what had once been Byra, although we searched everywhere. Could he have escaped?

We spread out to search in an ever-widening circle, but still there was no sign. Hope began to dawn in each of us. Just then, I heard what sounded like a faint groan. A couple of the poojarees near me had heard it too. We stopped to listen, but there was no other sound.

My companions, always superstitious, began to grow afraid. Three of us had clearly heard that groan. Some spirit must have made the sound. Maybe Byra's spirit. The two who heard cast fearful glances at me. A few moments more and perhaps they would take off.

Then I clearly heard the word 'Dorai'. It came very faintly, but there was no doubt about it. But from where? There was nothing in sight but grass and trees—and the big black rock.

The solution came in a flash. Byra was alive, and he was on top of that rock. How did he get there? Why, the elephant threw him there, of course!

I told my two companions the good news. In a trice they had clambered up the steep sides of the rock, and then we heard their joyful shouts: 'He's alive! Byra is alive!'

All of us grouped around the rock while the two men on top called out that Byra had said the elephant had thrown him up in the air. Luckily, he had fallen on top of the rock, where the beast could not get at him again. Had he fallen back to the ground, he would certainly have been crushed.

Then came bad news: 'His leg is broken, *Dorai*. Broken at the thigh.'

Removing my clumsy boots, I managed to get up the rock aided by my two companions pulling from above and others pushing from below. I found Byra with his thigh broken, but he was still smiling!

Possibly the elephant had seized him by the leg and broken the bone when it threw him. Perhaps falling on the hard rock was the cause. However, the all-important fact was that Byra was still alive. We made a stretcher out of branches, jungle-vines and soft, green leaves. As tenderly as we could, we moved him on to this. Meanwhile I sent for ropes from Kempekerai. Fastening these to the ends of the rough stretcher, we lowered him off the rock as gently as possible. Then we carried him back to the hamlet.

I had a difficult task to persuade Byra to let me take him to a hospital in Bangalore. He wanted to remain at Kempekerai until the ends of his broken thighbone joined.

Many jungle medicines and leaves possess marvellous healing properties. No doubt the end of the broken bone would unite. But would they join straight? Would Byra be able to walk normally again? I stressed these things and urged him to let me take him to hospital, but it was nightfall before I got his consent. The people of the forest are very afraid of our hospitals.

We set forth for Aiyur at break of day, willing hands bearing the stretcher, but it was very difficult to fasten the stretcher across the open box-*machan* that formed the body of 'Sudden Death,' my Model T Ford. At last it was done and by slow driving, avoiding the many potholes, it still took us a long time to reach the hospital at Bangalore.

There we created a sensation. Every doctor, nurse and ward-boy present, and every patient who could hobble and was not at death's door turned out to see the strange sight. It is not often that one comes across a car without a body, with no mudguards or driving seat, but with only an open box tied to it behind, and balancing precariously upon that open box a fragile stretcher of jungle wood, vines and leaves holding a small man, practically naked, with a broken thigh.

In four months Byra could walk as well as ever. The broken thighbone joined perfectly. The doctor said he had been a good patient. I know that the only thoughts that had sustained him throughout this period of pain and adversity were visions of his beloved jungles, and their mountains and streams.

It was a glad day when I took him back by car to Aiyur and walked with him to Kempekerai. We had to do it in slow stages. This time you may be sure I did not take Eric. For one I did not want to tempt the jinx that seemed to accompany this friend of my schooldays.

I almost forgot to relate that I was compelled to release the cobra I had caught two nights earlier when we were carrying Byra to the car. It would have been an added burden and a nuisance on the journey.

Two

The Medical Lore of India

THE POORER PEOPLE OF SOUTHERN INDIA CANNOT AFFORD TO GO TO a doctor to find cures for their ailments, for the very good reason that a single visit would take a large bite out of a week's earnings.

To give you an example: suppose a man has a sore or is suffering from a recent injury to a finger or leg, what would be the doctor's charges? Well, an injection of some sort would be indicated, probably antitetanus or penicillin in some form. Then there might be a dressing to be applied, together with tablets of some sulpha drug. The injection would cost at least, 1.50 rupees. The dressing and tablets another rupee. The doctor's professional fees would be around 3.50 rupees, so that the bill would be in the region of six rupees, a figure that represents three day's earnings at two rupees a day, if the patient is an unskilled labourer or a farmhand, and a full day's earning if he happens to be 'skilled'. So the ordinary man will think many times before going to a doctor.

So what does he do? He simply walks out on to the roadside where, within a few yards and in a minute or two he will undoubtedly come across a nice, warm flat mass of dung recently deposited by one of the many cattle that wander at will all over the streets and countryside. Our patient dips one or two of his fingers into the mess and comes up with a wet, sticky lump of dung which he applies to wound, tapping the same in smartly till it covers the whole surface of the injury in the shape of a small saucer.

That is all there is to it. Does it work? Incredibly it does in the great majority of cases. If, perchance, the treatment should fail and the wound not get better, or even gets worse, the reason (to the patient) is as plain as the nose on his face, and simple too. There was something wrong with the cow that passed the dung, and so sets out to repeat the treatment with another sample of excreta.

'But tetanus germs live in a cow dung' you exclaim. 'The medical books say so.' Undoubtedly they do, but you would have a real hard time getting that idea across to the patient. He would not believe a word of what you said, for one thing. For another, he would not believe there were such things as germs. When you tell him they are so small that he cannot see them with his eyes, he concludes the tale is a figment of your imagination or ignorance, deliberately told in order to frighten him into seeing a doctor. Very likely you are a doctor yourself.

Cobwebs of the species of spider that lives in holes in the ground, and those of the variety that spins its webs between the branches of small bushes, where they scintillate with multicoloured light-like clusters of jewels when the rising sun falls upon the dew that has gathered upon them, are sterling remedies when gathered freshly and plugged into freely bleeding wounds.

Juice from freshly broken pods of garlic is said to allay the irritation caused by mosquito bites, while for any form of eye trouble, the patient should stand facing the rising sun and squeeze orange-peel into his eyes. Equal quantities by weight of finely powdered indigo seeds and finely powdered tobacco leaf, put into the eyes at night, is reputed to cure cataract, although the patient is cautioned to expect some sensation of burning.

The bottle-bird or Indian tree sparrow performs a wonderful feat of architecture and tailoring when she builds her long, bottle-like nest of closely woven fibres and suspends it by a single strand from a tall date palm. After laying her eggs, the mother bottle-bird searches the landscape later in the evening, at an hour when she would otherwise be safely in her nest, for an early firefly or more than one firefly if she is lucky. Injuring the firefly sufficiently to prevent it from escaping but not seriously enough to kill outright, the wise little bird now introduces the insect into the nest through the cleverly constructed entrance that, strangely enough, is at its lower end.

What does our villager do when hurrying home unduly late of an evening and happens to notice the glow of the firefly through the interstices of a nest? He does not stop and climb the tree right away to break down the nest and procure the elfin within. That would take too long. He is already late and soon it will be quite dark. Moreover, he is alone. This is the hour when devils begin to emerge from their lairs beneath tombstones, from the trunks of *neem* and banyan trees, and from holes in the ground. In fact, the variety known as *minnispurams* are known to live in tall trees. Or, if he is near a jungle, there is the possibility of encountering a wild beast. So he makes note of the position of the tree in which the nest swings with its tiny lantern inside, and he hastens on his way.

The following morning he is back. Date palms are notoriously difficult to climb because of their thorny trunks and spiked leaf-tips. Our yokel therefore brings with him from the village a long bamboo pole, or if any grow nearby he proceeds to lop one of suitable length.

With this he brings down the nest by beating the single strand that secures it to a frond, and then he loses no time in extracting the firefly. That tiny glimmer is invisible now in the dazzling sunshine, but the villager knows it will shine again once the sun goes down and darkness covers the land.

He may keep it for good luck! Or he may eat it, for he reasons that the light will shine inside him, just as it shone in the nest, and will illuminate all the nooks and corners of his intestines so that the good spirit that looks after his welfare may be able to see and cure anything that is not quite right.

If young birds or eggs happen to be in the nest, he will throw them away with the rest of the nest, or if he is of a lower caste he might even eat the fledgelings.

Some of the wild creatures of this land are in great demand as medicine and are killed as soon as they are seen, if they are not lucky enough to get away. The black-faced grey langur monkey perhaps heads this list. Once common throughout the country, in southern India he has been slain mercilessly till the few of his kind that remain have moved into the innermost recesses of the forest. Even there they are shot by marauding bands of poachers, although their slaying is prohibited by the government. All this is being done in the belief that the flesh of a langur monkey is one of the most effective aphrodisiacs any failing male can hope to find.

Another unfortunate creature that is sacrificed to make medicine for the same purpose is the elegant Indian slender lorris, mistakenly called a 'sloth'. It is a pretty little monkey, delicately made, with no tail and two large, limpid brown eyes that reflect the rays of a torch as if they were made of pools of crimson fire. As it moves rather slowly, this poor creature is easily captured. Then its two eyes are torn out of their sockets while it is still alive to make a marvellous aphrodisiac for some man who has spent a lifetime in womanising and has reached a stage when he can womanise no more. The lorris, still alive but bereft of its two eyes and totally blind, is thrown aside to fend for itself. Unhappily, these little beasts possess a good deal of vitality and linger for days, till they eventually die of starvation.

Once I happened to find one in this state. I took it home, attended to its torn eye-sockets as best as I could, and fed it with milk. Despite its ghastly wounds the little monkey recovered.

For a long time it would not trust me, nor allow me to touch it, and bit viciously. But could anybody blame the tiny creature for being distrustful of human beings after the terrible ordeal it had suffered at their hands? Eventually, however, this little animal understood that I meant it no harm and was trying to befriend it. From that moment it changed its attitude towards me. No more affectionate and gentle little creature have I kept as a pet at any time.

A third mammal that suffers greatly in southern India because of a belief that may or may not have any foundation is the large Indian fruit bat commonly referred to as the 'flying fox'. The flesh of this mammal is reputed to be a very effective remedy for asthma, and as this complaint is widespread in the land despite its tropical climate, the flying fox is diligently shot, or netted, whenever the opportunity offers. However, in this instance the mammal is killed outright and the flesh cooked, as in the case of the langur monkey, and so it escapes the awful fate that befalls the slender lorris.

Snakes that are nonpoisonous also suffer a hard fate. The poisonous ones are killed and then burned (to prevent them from coming back to life), but the large and harmless snakes, as the *dhaman* or 'rat-snake' are skinned alive and then thrown aside. It is terrible to see the poor reptile, white without its outer skin, writhing and twisting in its agony. The outer skin is roughly cured with salt and copper sulphate and then sold for a couple of rupees to make a belt or purse, being unsuitable for making shoes unless it is fully tanned.

Doctors of another school speacialise in what they proudly call 'gem therapy'. This is the art of curing sicknesses by the use of semiprecious stones. It is performed in three ways:

1. Certain stones are burned to ashes and these ashes taken on the tongue or in water. The Ayurvedic System employs this method, but it is a practice of only the very rich.

2. A single stone—or perhaps a number of them—is soaked in water for a week, and this water is distributed, in half-ounce doses, as the medicine. Eleven jewels in particular are employed, namely the diamond, ruby, emerald, sapphire (both blue and white), moonstone, coral, cat's-eyes, gomed, pearl, amethyst and topaz. A twelfth, the opal, is made use of only in the case of eye ailments. A combination consisting of a number of these gems is allowed to 'cook' in water for a week. This water is then administered in small doses in cases of a more obstinate nature.

3. What is considered the highest form of gem treatment employs the principle of radiation and vibration. When a complaint is diagnosed and the gems that form the remedy are decided upon, the patient is seated directly in front of an electric fan, to the blades of which the required gem, or number of gems in little bags of netting are attached. The current is then switched on and the

blades made to rotate at high speed for fifteen or twenty minutes. The idea is that radiations of cosmic colour-force are thrown off from the gem or gems attached to the fan-blades directly upon the patient. This form of therapy is claimed to cure a sufferer from most long-standing complaints within a few weeks.

This therapy can also be used upon a patient residing miles away or in another country, even at the opposite end of the world. In such a case an object, intimate with person, is employed. it may be a photograph, a smear of blood upon blotting paper, a lock of hair, a fingernail or even handkerchief. This object, called 'the sample', is attached to a wooden frame which in turn is positioned six inches in front of the electric fan, to the blades of which the gems have been previously attached in small bags of netting. The current is switched on and the blades allowed to rotate at high speed for several hours, instead of just fifteen to twenty minutes, as when the patient is present in person. Astonishing cures have been reported.

But we have all heard of the Tibetan prayer-wheel which is used to rotate continuously with a prayer or a wish that has been enclosed within, while the petitioner concentrates upon it. He believes his wish will thus be granted, and very often it comes to pass. There could be connection between the crude revolving prayer-wheel and the revolving blades of the electric fan, of course, and the gems in their net-bags might simply be factors to aid the concentration of thought.

While the blades of the electric fan employ the principle of radiation, 'vibration' is used in employing an electric 'vibrator' or even a radio loudspeaker. The patient is seated directly in front of such a vibrator, upon which the selected gem or gems are placed and the current switched on, when the cosmic rays are said to be vibrated from the gems to the patient. Distant treatments are also undertaken in the same manner as with the electric fan. The patient's 'sample' is attached to a frame placed six inches in front of the vibrator. In some cases a variation is achieved by vibrating the 'sample' along with the gems in their net-bags, placing them all together upon the vibrator or at the centre of the loudspeaker's cones and switching on the current. For distant treatments, as in the case of the electric fan, the vibrator is made to work for some hours. The trembling vibration is said to impart the cosmic colour-force of the gems from the vibrator to the patient or his 'sample'.

These 'samples' as are said to represent the patient and to identify with him in all respects, no matter how far away he may be, and the radiations or vibrations falling upon them amount to those radiations or vibrations falling upon the patient directly.

Sometimes prayers or urgent wishes are written down upon a piece of paper and made to rotate on the blades of a fast-working fan for some hours or are placed upon a vibrator. Invariably these prayers or wishes become reality. In all instances the 'sample' or the piece of paper with the prayer or wish written upon it, absorb the cosmic rays thrown upon it or vibrated to it, and as these articles represent the actual person or the actual wish, patient gets cured even if he lives at the far end of the world, or the prayer becomes as actuality and is granted.

Space does not permit me to go into details, but I would like to give you a very brief résumé of this system:

Diamond. For energy. Prescribed in case of sterility, venereal disease, leucorrhoea, drunkenness, old age and all rundown conditions.

Ruby. Prescribed for cases of heart disease, headache, indigestion, sprue, eye diseases, loss of appetite and mental troubles.

Emerald. Prescribed in case of stammering, childishness, stomach disorders, the habit of telling lies, want of intelligence, mania, thieving, dumbness and deafness.

Pearl. Prescribed in cases of diabetes, tuberculosis, dropsy, diarrhoea, bladder diseases, jaundice, restlessness, vices of all sorts and a weak mind.

Coral. Prescribed for liver and blood diseases, measles, high blood pressure, piles, toothache, orchitis, diseases of the joints and urine troubles.

Topaz. Prescribed mainly for mental and personal lapses such as spendthriftness, hypocrisy, talkativeness, fondness for law suits, insanity, paralysis, rheumatism, diseases of the throat or palate and liver, obesity and tumours.

Sapphire. For cases of neuralgia, deformity, enlarged spleen, dropsy, hysteria, epilepsy and all forms of nervousness.

Gomed. For mental fears, suicidal tendencies, uterine troubles, constipation, diseases of the brain and glands, tumours and liver abcess.

Cat's-Eye. For boils, skin diseases, cancer fissure, itching, smallpox.

Opal. Mainly for all troubles involving the eyes.

The reader will undoubtedly be amused by the idea that gems might be able to effect any cure whatever, especially by the theory that 'radiation' or 'vibration' could be used on behalf of any patient thousands of miles away. But the proof of the pudding is in the eating, and there appears to be some justification.

From the beginning the government of India has not imposed a ban upon any of the many systems of medicine practised in this country, nor has any preference been shown officially for any particular practice. This policy was followed because of the numerous castes and creeds, some of whom have a marked liking for a particular system. The western systems are allopathy and homeopathy, from which we have the offshoots of elctro-homeopathy and Dr Schusscler's biochemical system of the 'twelve tissue remedies'.

The standard Hindu system is Ayurveda, in which the medicines are prepared from the leaves, bark, roots, seeds or flowers of herbs, plants and trees, with its sister system of Siddha, which is practically identical but practised chiefly in southern India. I can vouch for the efficacy of both these systems, which have claimed numerous successes where all other systems have failed.

Unani medicine is preferred by the Muslim community and depends for its ingredients not only upon plants, but upon minerals and precious stones as well. Chromopathy is followed by many, particularly in Hyderabad state (now Andhra Pradesh). A simple system, it employs the main colour of red, dark blue, sky blue, green, yellow and their intermediary blendings, to effect its cures. These colours are used in two ways. Glass bottles of different colours are filled to three-quarters of their capacity with plain water and allowed to 'cook' in brilliant sunlight for two days. An ounce of this water forms each dose of medicine. Along with this internal dose, the affected part of the human anatomy is exposed to coloured sunlight for twenty to thirty minutes at a time, the rays of the sun being allowed to shine upon the part through a sheet of glass of the required colour.

It is difficult nowadays to procure glass bottle, and even sheets or fragments of glass of the required colours or of their blends, so this snag is generally surmounted by purchasing transparent material like cellophane of the different hues, such as employed for making decorations.

This coloured paper is wrapped once, twice or thrice around a white glass bottle, according to the depth of colour required. Blends of colours are obtained by wrapping paper of first one colour and then another around the bottle; for example red paper, and then blue, to make purple. In place of coloured glass sheets, paper of the required hue is placed directly over the affected part, which is then exposed to strong sunlight.

You will probably think that chromopathy is a lot of nonsense, but I can assure you it is not.

We have all heard of diabetic carbuncles and of how difficult they are to cure, invariably requiring to be lanced. But let the sun shine on your carbuncle through blue glass or paper for thirty minutes twice a day, and at the same time drink four ounces of 'blue' water (water exposed to sunlight in a blue glass bottle or a bottle wrapped in transparent blue paper). Exposure to the sun must be done at noon and 3 p.m. when the days are at their hottest.

If you are anaemic, procure three large white glass bottles, wrap bright red, transparent cellophane twice around each, and tie the paper in position with red thread. Fill each bottle to three-fourths capacity with pure water and place the bottle in brilliant sunshine for two days. Mark the letters A, B and C on the corks of the respective bottles.

On the third day, finish the contents of bottle A in four or five doses. Refill the bottle immediately and place it back in the sunlight next day, while you drink the contents of the second bottle, marked B. Refill that and finish the third bottle, marked C, on the third day, refill it and put it back in the sun. On the fourth day, use the first bottle, marked A, once again, and so on. Your anaemia will begin to disappear in a week to ten days and the cost of treatment will have been the price of three sheets of transparent material.

To cure a wart or group of warts, procure a magnifying glass, wrap transparent yellow cellophane around it, and allow the sunlight to pass through the glass upon the wart, focussing the same to a point insufficiently concentrated to burn the skin. Expose the part from ten to fifteen minutes twice daily and the wart will shrivel up.

What is known as the 'urine system' is practised largely in the state of Gujarat. The basis of treatment is that the patient is kept on a low diet, amounting almost to complete fasting in some cases, and is given only his own urine to drink. No water, milk or other liquid is permitted. The system is prescribed for all complaints and is highly recommended in certain cases where allopathy and other methods have failed. Mr. Morarji Desai, a former Indian statesman, is a strong advocate of this system.

The 'de Chane system', originating in Hyderabad, is the skilful combination, by a very clever doctor, of the maxims of allopathy, homeopathy and Ayurveda. It has some astounding cure to its credit.

Diagnosis of complaints by the use of electro- or permanent magnets and a pendulum, or by plain intuition, is widely practised. Samples from the distant patient in the form of a bloodstain, a strand of hair, a silver or fingernail, a photograph or a bit of personal clothing act as substitute for the patient in his absence, and the operator not only correctly diagnoses the complaint from these substitutes without setting eyes upon the patient, but also indicates, according to whichever system of medicine the patient himself may prefer.

Healing by Yogic exercises, *pranic* breathing, relaxation and meditation are prevalent, while we have our quota of magnetic healers employing passes and the laying on of hands, or using autosuggestion and the direct spoken command to the genes and bodycells of the patient.

I have witnessed a practitioner of the last-mentioned system in action when treating a patient with severe dysentery. Laying one hand upon the patient's abdomen and the other on the small of his back, this practitioner almost shouted at the cells of the recalcitrant bowels to do their work properly, while at the same time addressing the genes in a cajoling, persuasive manner, telling them to instruct the wayward cells to do their duties properly. The dysentery stopped within twenty-four hours.

The reciting of mantrams, the performance of magical rites, the taking of oaths to give money or other gifts to some saint when a cure has been effected, are all forms of auto-suggestion that amount to self-hypnotism, a very important, and efficacious branch of the science of hypnotism, which again is a method of contact with the subconscious mind. The subconscious mind is the real centre of each one of us. It can accomplish any reasonable wish.

Black art is employed in India mostly for destructive ends but is also occasionally used for healing. It has always proved effective upon those who believe in it.

Cases of 'miracle' healing, under which heading I include religious healing, are often heard of, and the four great Indian religions—Hinduism, Islam, Christianity and Buddhism—claim successes in about equal numbers.

In giving this brief review of the general system of healing in use in India I have by no means covered all. Others remain that claim many cures. For instance we have the humble village soothsayer who corresponds to the medicine man of an African hamlet. This individual is the confidant of everyone, from headman and *patel* to the lowest *mochee* or cobbler, 'sweeper' and scavenger. He is called upon to heal any one of them when they are sick, to cure their cattle when bitten by snakes or rabid dogs, or their poultry when they get the

Ranikhet disease. He foretells periods of drought and when the monsoon rains will break, and even when floods are likely. He gives advice when crops fail. He helps in arranging marriages, settling disputes and quarrels over land, locates runaway wives and settles domestic problems. This nosey parker knows the business of everyone in the village. To what can we ascribe his general success? Are there hidden sciences and arts in which he is really a master? Or is he just exceptionally astute, a skilled psychologist, mind and character reader, a hypnotist to a degree and a smooth talker to a much greater degree? Or is he simply one who has a great deal of common sense and knows how to use it? But every villager will acclaim him his 'guru' (teacher).

Are there such things as 'secret potions' that can bestow good health, freedom from general sickness, perhaps from particular complaints? May be something that can bestow long life? Most people today will find this hard to believe, and about 'long life' I am not prepared to argue, having my own ideas on the subject. But I can tell you this much, and the information is culled from very ancient documents. There are three herbs that grow in India, and one in China, that are said to do just this. What's more, I have all three Indian varieties growing in my garden, while the Chinese plant, or rather an extract made from it, is available in Calcutta. But I can tell you for certain that there are herbs that keep away sickness, sustain the human heart, lower (or raise) the blood pressure, ensure against arteriosclerosis, cure asthma, diabetes, leprosy, leucoderma, rheumatism and many other complaints, and protect you totally against colds and 'flu.

I have a circular tin box filled with small blue glass bottles. Each contains one of these 'secret' herbs in powder form: I take a pinch from each of these bottles early in the morning and last thing at night and as far as possible carry this tin box with me wherever I go. People who have caught me in the act of swallowing these 'medicines' have been astounded at the number of them. And they have scoffed, but I am not perturbed. Touch wood (or my tin box), I just cannot catch a cold. The 'flu' lays out all the members of my household except myself at least twice each year. They get fever and various aches and pains, particularly when they are caught in the monsoon rains. I get soaked, too, and like it. I am sixty-three years old (1972) and can still walk a score of miles a day, especially in the jungle with the animals around me, and be fit for a few more.

For all of which, including the tin box and its contents, I thank God.

Three

Occult Lore and Other Matters

MATTERS OCCULT AND PERTAINING TO THE UNSEEN ARE TAKEN AS much for granted by the folk of southern India as are any of the material objects that they can see. Illness of any kind, a calamity, material losses or a spot of ill luck, whether of great consequence or small, are all ascribed to one of two causes. The first is the 'bad time' of the day (*rahukalam* as it is called), or maybe the 'bad time' of the recipient himself; the second is the deliberate machination of some evilly disposed enemy employing a black magician to cast a spell. In these circumstances, black magicians, spell removers (and those who cast spells), soothsayers and fortune-tellers of all descriptions are in great demand, and there never seems to be enough to go around.

In the larger towns, of an evening you will find these people seated cheek by jowl in long lines on the pavements. All kinds of fortune-tellers. Some employ a parrot or a lovebird which upon command from the owner, picks out certain playing cards from a pack or simply cards with fortunes inscribed in close lettering upon them.

Then there are fortune-tellers who ply their trade by consulting the cards directly or by throwing dice. The brotherhood of palmists is strongly represented. A few specialists tell fortunes by reading in the sand, or by charcoal marks on the pavement, or by studying the shadow thrown by the client at midday. Whatever their methods, none of them appear to want for clients, and as the fees range from one rupee to three for a consultation, the soothsayers seem to earn a very lucrative living.

It would be futile if you were to try to dissuade any of these clients from wasting their money. They would consider you a fool or an ignoramus. The Indian mind inclines strongly to the disposition of Fate, and the parrot or the lovebird, the playing cards, shadows and the rest are all agents that can be made to foretell one's future when handled by a skilled guru.

Most illnesses are ascribed to demon visitation, and for every patient who consults a qualified doctor, there is at least another—probably many more—who seek out 'medicine-man'. I have been a direct witness to many of these cases and the *modus operandi* is almost always the same. I will quote the case of young Niklas (Nicholas actually, but nobody appeared to be able to pronounce that word properly).

He was perhaps nineteen years old, rather short, very black with a handsome cheerful face, long wavy black hair and two rows of perfect teeth that showed prominently when he grinned, which was quite often. A pleasant, hard-working lad, he was popular with everybody up to the day his father was killed suddenly.

'Titch', the father, was what is known in India as a 'lineman'. He was employed by the Electricity department, and his duty was to be on hand at certain hours to answer emergency calls regarding electrical installations that went out of order suddenly. It was Titch's job to answer such calls and set the trouble right.

A call came through rather later one Thursday night, and Titch responded. Unfortunately, that Thursday happened to be the first of the month and Titch had drawn his salary earlier in the day. More unfortunately, Titch had been drinking. Not too much, but a little more than he should have, for Titch always celebrated payday with four or five shots of *arrack*. It did not cost much—about a shilling for two drams.

There had been a strong wind-storm about an hour earlier and the branch of a tree had fallen across the overhead cables, causing a short-circuit and some damage. It was pitch dark when Titch climbed the pole, and the miserably dim ray from the two-cell torch with its almost exhausted batteries supplied by the department hardly showed up the tangled wires. Just then it began to rain heavily and a sudden gust of wind set free the tangled wires from where they had been hanging, while the rainwater aided conduction. One wire fell across Titch's neck and the other almost missed his bare feet. Almost— but not quite! Seven thousand volts of electricity flashed through his body and Titch fell from the pole, bringing the wires with him. He was a ghastly sight two hours later after the storm had abated and they picked him up. The wire across his neck had burned its way into his flesh and he was a very dead man.

This event upset Niklas, but not nearly as much as his mother's conduct within the same month. She went to live with a neighbour, a young bachelor, for a week, and then the neighbour brazenly moved into the house that had belonged to Niklas's father, Titch, to live openly with the widow, Anthonyamma. All this shocked young Niklas, who spoke to his mother about it at the first opportunity. Was this how she respected the name and memory of her late husband, his father? Anthonyamma complained to her paramour, who threw Niklas out of the house that should have by rights been his and threatened to kill him should he dare to return.

Poor Niklas ran to his uncle, Arokiaswamy, for shelter, and the very next night had his encounter with a person who could have been none other than the Devil himself; or so the neighbours said. When I asked him about it, Niklas assured me he saw and spoke to this person as clearly as he was seeing and speaking to me at that moment.

There being no latrine in his home, Niklas had gone behind the nearest bush, as was the custom with all the members of the family, both male and female, in answer to the calls of nature. This had been at about nine o'clock at night, when it was quite dark. Ordinarily he would have been asleep by this time, but that night, for some reason, he did not feel sleepy. Niklas said he had been particularly careful, as it had rained an hour earlier and everyone knew that cobras came out of their holes in the ground to hunt for frogs after the rain.

He was down on his haunches when a tall man, dressed entirely in white, appeared before him. The man called him by name and bade him follow. Despite the position he was in at that moment, young Niklas had been impelled to obey and had followed behind the white figure, which maintained a distance of a dozen paces ahead despite Niklas' attempt to catch up. Another thing he had noticed was that the figure appeared to grow taller and taller but not to touch the ground.

They reached the great banyan tree that was growing half-a-furlong away, the figure in white still leading, before it finally halted. This enabled Niklas to catch up at last. He was not clear what happened next. At one moment the figure appeared to rise up vertically into the hanging roots of the old banyan. Then he could see it no longer. What he did recollect was a tremendous slap across the back of his neck, after which he remembered no more.

When Niklas failed to return, his cousin brought the fact to the notice of her mother and his uncle. Thinking nothing unusual, they had paid no attention till some time had passed. Then all three set out to look for the missing boy. The white shirt and pants Niklas had been wearing were what caught his aunt's eye, and they found him lying under the old banyan tree and carried him home. That tree was hundreds of years old and reputed to be haunted; therefore they reasoned that the lad's condition was clearly the outcome of some evil spiritual agency or agencies.

From that time on Niklas suffered from mysterious fits, at least once each day, and sometimes as many as three or four. These fits were not epileptic, as Niklas was never unconscious in their throes. In fact he spoke clearly, but in a language nobody could comprehend, though it appeared to concern his mother and her lover. He seemed, moreover, to be in towering rage during these attacks, for his eyes flashed and his teeth gnashed. He would become so violent that the combined efforts of all three persons in the household quite failed to control him. At times he would strike them or try to bite. At other times he would roll upon the ground, froth at the mouth and rave at everyone around him. Each attack lasted from ten to fifteen minutes. Then Niklas would return to normal slowly. It took about half-an-hour before he regained his composure. In a few days these attacks increased in intensity, becoming more frequent and of longer duration, while Niklas grew more and more violent.

It was quite late one night when my servants announced that he had just been summoned to come to Niklas, who had become unusually violent. The lad was some very distant relative of his, but in India nearly everybody is a relative, even if the relationship be removed seventy times seven. Besides, nobody ever misses the opportunity to delve into somebody else's affairs, particularly when such a good excuse as being a relative offers itself.

'Master would like to come?' invited my retainer. 'Tonight Debbil Man come all the way from city Market to drive away this *Pey* (evil-spirit). My mother's sisters' husband's brother's daughter's son pay him fifty rupees to drive debbil out of poor Niklas, who is son by second marriage to eldest brother of father-in-law of my cousin-brother, and therefore a close relative of mine.'

My senses reeled at the prospect of attempting to unravel Niklas' real relationship to my servant, but I supposed it could be done if sufficient tenacity was applied to the problem. But I am always interested in the occult and here was a chance of witnessing something special. Not that I thought this to be a genuine case of spirit obsession. There could be many other explanations, all of them mundane in character. Niklas could be putting on an act. I knew he hated his mother's new boyfriend. Perhaps he was afraid of this man when he had lived under the same roof with him. He might influence his mother to poison the man, or he might poison the man himself or poison the uncle who had befriended him. As likely as not, this was just a case of hysteria. Yet there might be something more to it.

'I'll come along,' I announced and soon we were both standing at the door of the tiny house occupied by Arokiaswamy, the uncle, and his family.

The place thronged with people and reeked with tobacco-smoke from numerous *beedies* (small native cigarettes wrapped in the leaves of the peepul-tree). Men and women were seated in a tight circle around Niklas, gaping to see what was going to happen next. Just then the boy appeared to be completely in his senses. He saw me enter the room, called a respectful greeting and invited me to come and sit next to him. With difficulty I climbed on the ground beside Niklas, opening the conversation by inquiring how he was.

Niklas answered that he was quite all right. Further conversation was interrupted by the entrance of the 'Devil Man' who was to exorcise the evil spirit.

He was a tall, cadaverous, very black individual, with unusually large eyes set in sunken sockets and great mop of black hair that surrounded his head like a woolly cap. He was dressed in a flowing black robe that reached to the ground. From looking at Niklas, his eyes fell upon me and he halted in his tracks. There was hostility in his looks and in the words that fell from his lips.

'What does the *Dorai* want here?' he asked arrogantly. 'If he is a preacher and wishes to pray, let him do so. If he is a doctor and has brought medicine, let him give it. I shall go.' With these words he turned back to the door, when many voices were raised to dissuade him from departing.

I got to my feet and called out: 'Let the driver-away-of-evil-spirits do his work in peace. I came but to see the lad, and having seen I shall return.'

The black magician (for such he was and as such I shall allude to him in the rest of this story) appeared mollified: 'Let the *Dorai* remain and watch me drive out the spirit, if he so wishes. I know all white men are consumed with curiosity regarding such things. Only he must not interrupt me by word or deed.'

'I shall not,' I promised, and sat down in my former place by the side of Niklas.

The black magician advanced, seated himself directly before Niklas and summoned his uncle Arokiaswamy, a lanky middle-aged individual, to bring the black cock and the bottle of *arrack* that had already been procured for the ceremony.

When the liquor and the trussed fowl were handed to him, the magician drew a dirty-looking pocketknife from the recesses of his clothing, unfolded the blade and began to saw the throat of the unfortunate bird with its blunt edge. The cock began to flap its wings but the magician continued till he had completely severed the head from the body. The thick red blood that gushed from the stump contrasted strongly with the cock's black feathers. The magician allowed a small quantity of this blood to run into a diminutive aluminium drinking mug, while the rest of it dripped on to the dry earthern floor of the hut and was absorbed.

From his pocket he brought out some dry resinous powder wrapped in paper and allowed it to spill on to the floor. The magician borrowed a match from me and set fire to the powder after several attempts. It burned with a greenish flame. Then he picked up the aluminium mug and held it over this flame for a few seconds while he closed his eyes and started muttering incantations in a singsong voice. I noticed that the green flame burnt itself out pretty soon but the magician continued with his mantras.

At last he finished, opened his eyes and, lifting the mug, ordered Niklas to drink. The lad appeared to be in some kind of a trance. His eyes were open but turned upwards, so that I could see the whites. His lower jaw was slack and partly open, and he was rocking himself backwards and forwards to the rhythm of the magician's droning voice. He stretched out his hand obediently and the magician placed that mug in his grasp, closing the boy's fingers firmly around the vessel so that he would not drop it.

Once again he commanded 'drink', and at one gulp Niklas swallowed the hot red blood.

The magician now seized the boys's right wrist in his left hand, and left wrist in his right hand, and raising his voice, commenced shouting the vilest obscenities at the evil spirit said to be within the lad, calling it strings of unmentionably bad names and commanding it to be gone forthwith.

Niklas started to twist and to turn and then to struggle violently with the man who was holding him down, but the magician clung to his wrists and shouted further abuse upon the demon within, commanding it to come forth at once.

Niklas became more violent; then he started to scream aloud. But his shouts were coherent: 'Go away from here. Why do you torment us? We have no place to live and you are ordering us out of the only shelter we have been able to find for so long.'

The words almost turned into a plea. The magician released Niklas' wrists to enable himself to fill the aluminium mug to the brim with raw liquor from the bottle, and tossed the contents down his own throat. He quickly repeated this action, then laid the mug down, grasped the boy's wrists once more and recommenced ordering the demon to leave Niklas.

The lad started to struggle violently, so much so that the magician was compelled to call upon some members of the assembly to help. While this was being done, he did not lose the opportunity to fortify himself still further with yet more *arrack*. Things came to a head a moment later when Niklas gave vent to a piercing screech, jumped to his feet in spite of the many pairs of hands that were holding him, and then fell to the ground as if poleaxed. He kicked spasmodically a few times, stretched his body tautly while grinding his teeth (which sound we all could hear), then threw his arms above his head and ceased to move.

A low wail came from the audience. Clearly most of them thought the boy was dead, but as I watched his chest I could detect rise and fall of his breathing.

The magician was now pointing dramatically to the corner of the room where the light from an oil-lamp hanging from a nail on the wall could barely reach. 'Do you see them?' he quavered. 'Not one spirit, but two. A man and a woman.'

Everyone looked in the direction he was pointing. Of course, nothing could be seen, but the people seated nearest to that corner scrambled hastily to their feet and backed away.

Sensing he was master of the situation, the magician then started to engage in a garbled argument with the spirits that only he could see and hear.

'No, you shall not come back,' he yelled. 'No, not even if you pay me a thousand rupees. These are poor folk. The miserable advance they have paid me for my services is but a pittance. I know they will pay me much more before I leave, so I won't take any part of the one thousand rupees you are offering me.'

'Stand aside,' he ordered. 'Stand away from the doorway. The two spirits are leaving now. Can't you see them? A man and a woman; both completely naked. The woman is very beautiful. She is bedecked with jewels. She has a very pretty face and a lovely figure, but she is evil—very, very evil. For the woman is a devil, you must know.'

'Stand aside,' he continued while the crowd, and particularly the menfolk, began to gape in the hope of a glimpse of this lovely, naked girl. 'Stand, I say. For if she gets within reach of you she may change her mind about leaving and enter into you instead, then you will know all about it.'

There was a general stampede to the opposite side of the room, which being filled with people already, caused considerable pushing and shoving. At that moment my eye caught the magician's. I could swear there was a twinkle of laughter in his. He seemed to be saying to me: 'If people want to be fooled so easily, let me fool them. Don't spoil things.' So I remained a silent spectator.

'Ah, now they are leaving' went on the magician. Then, after a moment, 'They have left. Now nobody should go outside for at least half an hour to allow the spirits to get clear away.' As a result, I was obliged to remain another thirty minutes in that congested room. It would not have been fair to leave earlier and let the magician down.

This may well have been a farce from start to finish; I agree. Niklas was either an accomplice and played his part well, or this was a simple case of hysteria, since his mother's conduct had upset him greatly. And as Niklas had gained nothing by acting, so we must conclude that Niklas' subconscious mind, in a tremendous state of frustration at being turned out of his own home, wanted to draw attention to his own unenviable position in the new household that his mother had set up with her boyfriend. The fact remains, however, that from that time Niklas was completely cured. He never again suffered from fits and all the credit went to the black magician, the driver-out-of-evil-spirits, for his wonderful performance. We may regard the whole performance as a smart bit of work, but no other person living in these regions will agree: it was to them clearly and simply a case of possession by evil spirit.

Now let me relate the story of Maria, which is far more difficult to explain. Of course, I cannot give you the lady's real name, but Maria will serve the purpose. She was an Anglo-Indian of slightly less than middle age, respectably married, with four children. A good housewife and a hard worker, she did not care for servants whom she maintained were more a hindrance than a help. And she abhorred mendicants.

Now if there is anything for which India is notorious, it is its beggars ; they swarm everywhere. They throng the roads and accost you in the market-place, and as if that is not enough, they call at your front door and will not go away till you give them alms.

Many such mendicants were in the habit of visiting the house where Maria lived, and among them was one in particular who annoyed her immensely. He was a tall, very black man with long hair and a great black beard that streamed down over his chest. He had the most piercing black eyes she had ever seen. This fellow generally wore the accepted costume of a yogi; a long saffron robe reaching to the ground. It was far from clean, as was also the saffron cloth he wore loosely around his head as an untidy turban. Caste marks of white and red on his forehead, a necklace of large amber beads and a stout staff completed his dress. He was always barefooted.

Maria detested the fellow for two reasons. The first, his arrogant manner of demanding alms. Here was no beggar, he made one feel, but someone whose demand had better be met or ... The second reason was more subtle. The man's piercing black eyes seemed to Maria to undress her each time he looked at her. It made her feel as if the clothes she wore— she was invariably a chic dresser—might just as well be dispensed with for all the good they did in hiding her nakedness.

One day Maria was particularly busy and the beggar particularly demanding, with the result that she ordered him to get out. Resenting this, the mendicant argued back, when, true to the habits of almost all Anglo-Indians in this hot country, Maria started to abuse him in no uncertain manner.

The response to this was quite unexpected. The visitor said not a word but just glared at her, and those terrible eyes of his seemed to grow larger and to come closer and closer. Now they appeared but a few inches away, and as Maria stood rooted to the spot, they came yet nearer and the next instant were inside her. Or so it seemed.

A still small voice now spoke to her. It was not that of the magician's which was deep and sonorous. This was a high-pitched, treble voice, the sort of voice one would associate with a boy of eight years or so. And it always laughed before it said anything. Maria was to come to know of this to her cost very soon. Always that high-pitched, cackling, treble laughter before the words came.

'At last,' chortled the childlike voice, 'I have managed to get back into a human body. It has been so many years, so many long years. But at last I have succeeded. You are mine, Maria, and I will never let you go.' The words rose to a crescendo. 'Never will I leave you, nor will I let you leave me, Maria. From this day forth we two shall be one. Husband and wife, my dear. It has been such a long, long time.'

Maria told me this story afterwards and said that from that moment all sense of privacy was lost to her. Never, at any moment, did she feel alone. 'The Voice,' as she called it, was always with her day and night and it was particularly the nights that she dreaded.

As time passed, this demon within her began to make itself more and more felt. It would always be talking to her in its high-pitched, treble voice, making the most obscene suggestions. Worse still it was always laughing. When she undressed or took her bath, it would scream with glee and shout, 'I can see you! I can see you!' When she lay down to sleep at night it would say the filthiest things to her and make the most vulgar suggestions, ending with 'I want you. I must have you.'

Matters grew worse as the Voice began to make its demands more and more pressing. Maria would awaken with a start, a sense of a heavy weight upon her as if somebody was lying on top of her. At other times she would feel herself clasped tightly in a pair of strong invisible arms.

Gradually Maria began to change in her own conduct and nature. She had always been an upright person of good character, but I expect the continuous flow of lewd suggestions and the actions that these suggestions awakened wore Maria down till she herself started to welcome, and finally follow, those continuous promptings. By this time the people who had known her and noticed the change began to talk about it, and in our town rumours spread rapidly.

Thus it was that I came to hear of Maria, and being always interested in such matters, lost no time in contacting her through the friend who had told me.

Maria did have short respite now and again from the prompting of the Voice, although this was not very often or for long. Luckily, it was on one of those occasions that I first met her and I had time to gain her confidence and hear her story before the Voice suddenly came back and took hold of her. There was no mistaking this, for Maria abruptly stopped speaking to me in mid-sentence and her voice changed to an almost childlike treble lisp: 'How nice of you to visit me. Do come and sit closer, it will be so cosy for both of us.'

Maria was handsome in appearance and of pleasing build and it was easy to understand how her change in habits and her newly acquired intimate and sexy behaviour was going to get her into a lot of trouble. The friends who had told me about her and probably nearly all those who had heard the story were convinced hers was a clear case of possession. The mendicant whom Maria had ordered away so abruptly had laid a curse upon her, one of the worst curses that can be put upon anybody in the East: the curse of obsession by an evil entity or spirit. Millions of people believe in this sort of thing. The events clearly pointed to it. There could be no other possible explanation, they would say.

I have travelled a lot in India in my time, during which period I have never lost an opportunity to investigate, as far as possible, every case of occult happening that has come my way. I have read a lot about these things, met and spoken to a number of black magicians and delved into the matter as deeply as I could. Indeed, I have gone as far as to become initiated into the cult of black magician by preforming certain rites that, under the oath of secrecy, I cannot reveal.

Anyone who has delved into these matters deeply enough and gained sufficient experience develops a sort of uncanny sense for knowing whether a case he may encounter is actually the result of a black magician's spell or not. As I have said already, nearly everything of an abnormal kind that happens in India is attributed to the occult and to black magic, but to those who, like myself, have studied the subject, this is far from being so. A fair percentage of people who suddenly begin to act queerly do so for quite natural reasons. Hysteria plays a very large part in the lives of people in the East, both men and women, but more particularly among women at the time of menstruation and menopause.

Then again, people in the East are far more emotional then those in the West. Little injuries done to them assume gargantuan proportions, and they brood and brood over their wrong till, quite frequently, their minds give way. At best, there is but a narrow margin in the minds of us all between sanity and insanity, and it does not take very much or very long for that small barrier to break down and the same to become insane, at least to some degree or in certain ways. So before attributing anything to occult influence, we should not fail to consider whether suggestion and autosuggestion may have played a part in influencing the person concerned to act in a given manner. Repeated and powerful suggestions upon the subconscious mind of practically any ordinary individual will soon cause that person to act in the way intended while hypnotism, which is after all but a well-harnessed form of suggestion, undoubtedly acts as a most powerful factor.

Hypnotism, powerful and almost instantaneous, is an art well-known and widely practised in India by some pseudo-yogis and other interested persons, and I felt certain Maria's case fell entirely into this category. She had repeatedly stressed that the mendicant's piercing black eyes seemed to bore right through her, to undress her, as she said, to the point that she felt it was useless for her to wear any clothing. His gaze and his concentrated silence had brought her under his hypnotic influence undoubtedly, and she was but carrying out in practice the suggestions he had forced upon her.

The only solution was to break that hypnotic spell, but to do so successfully would require an indirect approach. I knew it would be useless for me to tell her that she had been hypnotised and that I would try to remove the hypnotic influence that had been brought to bear upon her. Without doubt, one of the first commands her visitor had given her under his spell was to resist any suggestion that he was influencing her. I would have to hypnotise her myself without her knowing what was happening, and then put the counter-suggestions required to nullify the orders of the mendicant.

Luckily I was wearing my heavy silver ring, set with a blue stone, a gift to me from a close friend from Ghana, so I decided to play upon Maria's clear belief that she had been bewitched by using this belief to hypnotise her.

'Maria,' I began, 'I am wearing a ring that has come all the way from Ghana in Africa. It belongs to a very powerful witch-doctor who gave it to me. Now, if you will stare at the blue stone on this ring without closing your eyes, I will invoke the magic that is in the ring to free you of your trouble for all time.'

Maria was a simple sort of woman, obviously not well read, and the mendicant's suggestion in the form of the Voice continued its cackling, followed with a lewd suggestion each time, for many minutes, while I persisted with my magic ring. But at last she quietened down and agreed to look at the ring. Removing it from my finger, I laid the ring upon a small table that I placed close before her.

I asked her to stare at it without blinking her eyes. Maria then started to do as I had asked.

At first her gaze would wander, but I brought it back each time till I finally succeeded in rivetting her attention upon the blue stone. Slowly I made the sleep suggestion and in a surprisingly short while Maria was sound asleep under my hypnotic influence.

The rest was easy. I made the counter suggestions required to nullify the mendicant's earlier commands and continued for some time, till I felt my orders had supplanted the mendicant's earlier evil commands. I told her that never again would she be troubled by the Voice. That had been only her own imagination. She had never heard any such voice. There never had been a voice. It had been a nasty dream. Entirely her own imagination. No such thing as a Voice! I then woke her up.

The lady, as I have told you, was basically a good woman and I am glad to be able to record that she was quite cured from that moment. No longer did she hear the high-pitched treble voice (which, incidentally, was her own voice pitched to a treble key under hypnotic instruction), urging her to do and speak obscene things. No longer did it speak to her night and day. Maria had been freed and neither the devil nor any evil spirits had played any part in entering into her.

Nevertheless, I have come across some well-authenticated cases of spirit-possession and I will now tell you about one of these. I have already mentioned the case of Ossie Brown in some detail in my earlier book, *The Call of the Man-Eater*. The story begins in much the same way as Maria's. A fakir in a yellow robe was wont to present himself on the first day of every month at the pay-counter of the premises where Ossie was working and demand alms from him and the other members of staff as they received their salaries.

In time, Ossie resented this peremptory attitude and threatened to hand the man over to the police. Hot words followed, ending with the fakir cursing Ossie and a statement that he would put 'someone' into my friend who would take up his abode there and remain till death.

That very night Ossie awoke with the curious sensation that he was not alone. He opened his eyes to see a dark figure outside his mosquito net. The figure came closer and closer and appeared to merge with him by actually getting inside him. Thereafter, Ossie started exhibiting strange mannerisms at work. His voice and behaviour would change. Apparently he did not know where he was, or who he was. He would ask gruffly how he came to be there. Then he would walk out of the room. Sometimes he would return after a lapse of thirty minutes or an hour quite oblivious of his behaviour or of how he left his work spot. Occasionally he would collapse, as if in a fit. When he recovered, he was quite normal and was very surprised at being told of his behaviour.

Just about this time, rather foolishly, I invited Ossie on a trip to the jungle. We camped that night on the banks of a great river, far from human habitation. A herd of wild elephants was grazing close by. We could hear them trumpeting and breaking the branches off trees, and we lit a large camp fire to keep away any stray elephants that might come our way.

Suddenly, a strange gruff voice addressed me, demanding to know who I was. It came from Ossie, but as I looked at him I saw quite another person looking back at me. The eyes, the face, everything was different. This entity repeated his demand. Who was I? Where were we?

I tried to pacify Ossie by saying we had come out shooting, whereupon he demanded that I should give him my gun. Fortunately, he did not notice that my rifle was against a tree directly behind him. I knew that if he got hold of it he might shoot me. So distracting his attention to the elephant, I pounced upon the weapon and threatened to shoot him if he came any closer.

Regardless of my threat, he advanced upon me. I knew only too well that in a physical struggle I would be no match for this person, evil spirit or not. I would be compelled to shoot and at least wound my friend and that would not be an easy thing to do with a heavy calibre .405 rifle.

When he was only five feet away the solution came to me. I fired the rifle so that the bullet just whizzed over his head. Ossie halted abruptly, shuddered and passed a hand over his forehead wearily. The next second the possessing entity had gone and my friend spoke to me in his normal voice.

The sequel to this story is that Ossie went to Calcutta where, one day, he threw himself from the second floor of a building and was killed. To me this case was a clear example of spirit-possession. You will notice it differed from Maria's in one very important fact. Maria fancied she heard a voice in her own head telling her to do things. She did not change or act differently herself. By that I mean her personality remained the same. In Ossie's case the change was in himself, physically as well as outwardly. His manner, appearance and voice all changed in the twinkling of an eye. Secondly, Maria could always remember what the inner voice, prompting her, had said. In Ossie's case he was quite ignorant of all that had happened to him and could remember nothing.

The reason for the difference appears obvious. Maria's conscious and subconscious minds were overshadowed by the orders of the mendicant, delivered while she was under hypnosis and in his control. Nevertheless it was Maria's own conscious and subconscious minds that were functioning under the orders of an outsider disguised under an assumed identity of a childlike, treble voice. With Ossie, both his conscious and subconscious minds were not only dominated, but temporarily taken possession of by quite another identity, this time a discarnate entity under the orders of the fakir, who must have been a powerful medium as well as master of black magic. As a result, Ossie's conscious and subconscious minds were not functioning at all at the time and so he remembered nothing of what had taken place.

There are quite a number of persons living in India today who perform each day, and sometimes several times in the course of each day, the miracle of what are known in spiritualistic parlance as 'the phenomenon of apports'.

In the darkness, or the dim red illumination in the seance room, spiritualists claim that small objects such as flowers or other trivial articles are brought to them by the spirits and laid upon their laps even though all doors and windows have been closed. The mystics of India go much farther than this. To begin with, they operate in broad daylight, in an open space, sometimes with hundreds of people looking on.

Sai Baba the reincarnated, generally referred to as Sathya Sai, who is a personal friend whom I have known as a lad and who claims to be the reincarnation of the original Sai Baba the great who died many years ago, once stretched out his hand in front of me and closed it over a little metal image which appeared to materialise and his fingers were closing upon it! Baba, as he is affectionately referred to by his personal acquaintances, gave it to me as a keepsake and I put the little figure in my purse.

Years later a pickpocket relieved me of this purse, with my money and the figurine inside, as I was boarding the last night-bus from Bangalore to Whitefield, twelve miles away, where I was living at the time. I knew nothing of the theft at the time, but about halfway to my destination the conductor came round collecting tickets. I put my hand into my pocket for my purse.

It was gone! Worse still, I did not have another coin on my person.

Yet there was something small and hard in the corner of that pocket. I felt again and drew out the small figurine that Baba had given me. It had been inside one of the compartments of the missing purse. The purse itself had been taken. How had the little image come back into the pocket?

The conductor was looking hard at me. Suspicion came into his face when I withdrew my hand, empty except for the tiny figure between my fingers. The conductor pulled the cord to stop the bus. We were about seven miles from Whitefield and it was five minutes to midnight. Moreover, it was raining. I had the prospect of a long walk before me.

I explained that my pocked had been picked. The conductor grinned sardonically; 'Tell that to the Marines,' he said in the local dialect. Only, having never heard of the Marines, he used another name in its place, a very rude word with a very, very dirty meaning that I cannot possibly repeat. Then his eyes fell upon the figurine. His manner changed. He pulled the cord twice, which was the signal for the driver to proceed.

'We'll risk it,' he said. 'No inspector is likely to check at this time of night.'

I thanked that conductor when I alighted from the bus. He confided that he was a devotee of Baba's. I have often wondered whether Baba, when he produced the figurine out of the air that day and gave it to me, knew what good purpose it was to serve in saving me from a long, wet, midnight walk.

The second time I went to Baba was when I was in a spot of real trouble. Before I could ask him, he told me my trouble. He also told me what were to be the consequences. He gave me that answer nearly thirteen years ago and everything he said came to pass exactly. Before parting, he stretched out his hand for me to shake. As he did so, I noticed that he closed his fingers over something. Then he handed me a small piece of ash.

'Keep it in a small box, carefully,' he advised. 'Should you have any trouble at any time, or a problem, open the box and look upon the ashes. Picture my face in the ashes. I think your trouble, or problem, whatever it is, will disappear very soon after that.'

I did exactly as Baba had told me. I cannot say I have been trouble-free. But whatever my trouble, they have since turned out to be but little ones. And I still have that box with the ashes in it.

However, this is a digression. The question is, how do people like Baba get these apports? There seem to be only two solutions. The first is obvious. Trickery, in the form of sleight-of-hand. Something that our fathers, grandfathers and great-grandfathers have seen on the stage for years. The second solution defies explanation.

Let us consider trickery first. Did Baba successfully 'palm' the figurine and the ashes upon me, right under my nose, without my noticing how he did it? I deny it, but what is the use of arguing? So let me tell you some of the other occurrences which he brought to pass. You will then be in a better position to judge whether 'palming' could have been possible.

A sick girl was brought to him. She had been suffering from a permanent headache for months. By apport, Baba produced a small bottle of very strongly scented balm. The first application of this balm upon her forehead cured that headache for good.

Baba was once invited to an alfresco tea-party. The tables were spread beneath a grove of large and beautiful mango trees. The month was November. No fruit grows on mango trees in November. April to June are the months for mangoes in India.

Somebody remarked, 'What a pity there are no mangoes now.' To which Baba replied, 'But there are.' In his hand was a stalk, to which three ripe mangoes and a couple of leaves were attached.

One more incident. Baba was travelling by car from Bangalore to his permanent abode in Puttaparthi. Short of his destination by about fifty miles, the car stopped. The driver had not put sufficient petrol into the tank. They would either have to beg some passing lorry for petrol, or Baba must go by bus for the rest of the journey.

Baba stepped out of the car, walked to the rear and stretched the palm of his hand over the petrol tank. Then he reseated himself. 'Drive on,' he instructed. 'We now have enough petrol to complete the journey.' And they had.

So, if these things are not done by sleight-of-hand, how are they done? At least, how do people in India say they are done?

There are two current explanations. Basically, they amount to the same thing, although in *modus operandi* they are quite dissimilar. The general opinion is that the apports are brought to the master desiring them through the agency of what are known as 'Kutti shaitans', diminutive little sprites generally invisible, but which at times take on the appearance of tiny, naked, very black people, no more than six inches in height and of both sexes. The number of *Kutti-shaitans* in the band that serves him or her depend on the degree of occult power possessed by the master and it may vary from a single one to two dozen.

Elaborate methods are prescribed as to how a person may gain control over one or more of these little elfs, but they are said to be quite dangerous people once you have anything to do with them. The trouble is that when you set yourself to acquire one or more of them, they in turn acquire you and the contract is for life; you cannot revoke it at any period, and if you try to do so the direst of repercussions await you in the form of great misfortune, sickness and eventual death. Moreover, the sprites do not serve you for nothing: they will obey you and get you what you want, provided you in turn agree to their terms and give them what they want. And their terms and wants are always of a horrid nature.

Once a week, mostly on Fridays, but with some magicians on Thursdays, time must be set apart at midnight on which these payments are to be made to the little sprites in a room specially appointed for the purpose. Blood is frequently demanded: pig's blood, the blood of a black cock, human blood from a vein in your own or somebody else's arm, or menstrual blood. Sprites of a lower order demand that you commit the greatest sacrilege against the dictates of your own religion, whatever it may be, by saying things, doing things and submitting religious objects to deeds that are the most blasphemous possible.

Nor is that all. No master may marry. If he wants to cohabit with a woman he must first get permission from his Kutti shaitans to do so. This is only bestowed after incurring a heavy penalty. Financially, the master can never be in abundant circumstances. He will receive only enough money to live in moderate comfort. Never may he become rich.

To acquire one of these sprites, he must first become a black magician of which there are many orders. Actually to capture the sprite he is required to visit a buffalo-kraal at midnight on the night of the Amavasa, which is the darkest night of the month, exactly halfway between full moon and the succeeding new moon. He should hide himself in a corner of the kraal along with the buffaloes, arriving at least an hour before midnight. When the time comes and the hour strikes, if he looks earnestly enough he will generally notice something rather like a big moth or a small bat flitting about on the back of one of the buffaloes. The seeker should approach it quietly and make snatching motions with his arms and hands, as if trying to seize this flitting creature.

Of course he would never really be able to seize a sprite. His motions are only symbolical and signify his earnest desire and intention to succeed.

The sprite, or Kutti shaitan, will then speak to him, normally by means of mental rather than spoken conversation.

'What are you trying to do?' it will ask.

'I mean to capture you,' the seeker will reply.

'Why? What do you want of me?' the sprite will ask.

'I mean to catch and conquer you. I want you for my servant; to do my bidding and get me whatever I may desire.' The seeker is required to be very firm and positive in this assertion.

The sprite may remonstrate at first, or begin to bargain straightaway. Often it may lay down extremely difficult, if not quite impossible, conditions in return for its services. The seeker is strongly advised to refuse straightaway and then to try to drive as hard a bargain as possible, for he must remember that, once it is made, the pact is sealed for the rest of his lifetime. It may never be broken, renounced or cancelled. Many instances are on record of black magicians who, for one reason or another, but principally for the sake of contracting a marriage, have tried to nullify their agreements with their

Kutti-shaitans, either by straightforward renunciation or trickery. The direst penalties have befallen them in the way of misfortune, sickness, loss of sight or limbs, or even death. So you should really think twice before you enter into an agreement of this sort, even if it is your own self that is able to bring you so many nice things.

The other common belief, and this is more prevalent in northern India than in the south, is that the familiar who brings the apports, and is known by the name of the *hamzad*, is merely your own astral self, resembling you in every way, including appearance, mannerisms and even clothing. The *hamzad* is believed to be capable of travelling to the ends of the earth in the twinkling of an eye, of carrying enormous weights and of being able to do anything for you and get you whatever you want. It is understood of course that everything the *hamzad* brings is made invisible in course of transit and is made to resume its substantial appearance when the *hamzad* presents it to his master.

You are required to work hard before you can capture the services of your *hamzad*. This is done by following certain very secret formulae. As in the case of the Kutti-shaitan, a two-way bargain must be entered into between the seeker and his *hamzad* for service to be rendered and this bargain is mandatory for life. Penalties of the most frightful character, including the violent termination of the seeker's life, follow the breaking of this pact by the human partner.

It may be interesting to note certain fundamental differences as well as some basic similarities, between western black magic and the Indian brand of black magic.

The main difference seems to lie in the fact that, European black magicians, generally known as wizards and witches, more or less make undisguised covenants with Lucifer, the spirit of the morning, and other terms synonymous with

Satan, or more commonly, the devil; the Indian black magician will very stoutly deny that the devil ('shaitan' being the name in Hindi and 'pey' or 'pisachee' in Tamil) plays any part in the bargain. Kutti-shaitans, or the *hamzad* or, on some occasions a particular spirit variously known as a '*minispuram*' in the south and in western India as a 'raksha', are the entities invoked for this purpose and they are by no means considered to be devils, nor do they bear any resemblance to one. The Indian seer firmly believes that he is dealing with one or more very powerful spirits who are definitely not of an evil disposition, although they may at times be tempted or driven to outbursts of the most severe anger or revengefulness, or plain malevolence. He will very strongly deny that he is having any truck with the devil and will become most indignant if you insist that this is so.

At the same time, considering that the aims of the two schools are about the same, while the result attained are more or less equal, one cannot but wonder whether the devil or any other spirit, has really anything to do with it. Of course, the westerner will claim that the devil and the *minispuram* or spirit are one and the same. The Indian will stoutly deny it: his *minispuram* is far from being a devil.

Maybe, however, the much maligned devil and the greatly feared *minispuram* have nothing whatever to do with it, and that it is the black magician's, or the witch's own subconscious mind that is at the bottom of the whole affair, assuming and playing the part of the devil or the *minispuram,* just to satisfy its owner?

It will be noticed that in all cases a bargain is mandatory. Without this pledge on the part of the black magician on the one hand and the entity on the other, no deal can transpire, no pact may be made. Why is this so? The religious-minded person will claim that by striking a pact of this kind, the devil will win over the witch's soul to himself, with eventual damnation and hell. The black magician of India will say that his *minispuram* must naturally require, and receive, some sort of reward and satisfaction for his labours on his master's behalf.

May it not also be a fact that the existence of a pact serves to remind the magician always of his contacts with the other side, the devil or spirit who is under an obligation to him and to whom he is equally beholden every moment of the day and night? The pact serves to rivet the attention of conscious and subconscious minds at all times.

Therein lie the essential ingredients that make black magic work: the strong awareness on the part of both the conscious and subconscious minds of the magician, western or eastern, that he has struck a bargain with some supernatural power possessing the attributes of ability and willingness to work for him with assured success, and get him what he wants, in return for the possession of his very self. The magician and this power thus become welded into one force, as it were, and this thought is with him at all times, giving him a boost of selfconscious assertiveness and confidence in himself that he would not normally possess.

Conversely, all self-assertiveness and self-confidence completely disappear in a victim in India, even if he should by nature have these attributes, when he finds himself pitted against a black magician. Generations of upbringing together with the frightening tales drilled into him from childhood, make him quite certain that he is absolutely helpless before the man of magic and is entirely in his power.

Thus we have a person all filled with confidence in a supernatural power that is helping him day and night, opposed to another who has known from childhood that he is helpless against a foe who has supernatural assistance. The result is a foregone conclusion and the man of magic always wins.

Latent hypnotism plays a major part in both the casting and removal of 'spells' in India. Everyone has heard of 'mantras' and 'mantrams', words used in relation to magical formulae of one kind or another. The words are identical in meaning and apply to everything from coherent sentences, uttered either in ancient Sanskrit or in the local vernacular (it should be remembered that there are about three hundred vernaculars in use throughout India and Pakistan) in either prose or poetry, to incoherent and meaningless phrases. Mantras are employed to bring good luck, employment, a suitable partner in marriage, a male child, protection against sickness or danger, a cure for any sickness and for a host of other purposes. In fact, their employment is practically synonymous with the use of talismans, but with a rather wider range.

It is the repetition of such a mantra, over and over again, that serves to focus the attention upon a particular purpose or objective. It serves to keep the mind from straying away from that purpose or objective. Thus one attains a determination, together with a large degree of autosuggestion, which in itself is nothing but auto- or self-hypnotism.

A third factor is also present ; a great impelling desire, coupled with great personal emotion. The person is all worked up, in all his being, to achieve and to acquire what he wants. So we have here the ingredients necessary for attaining success in any field. Firstly determination, the great driving factor; secondly, a great desire to attain it, a sort of burning need for it; thirdly, belief or faith that what is being striven for will be achieved; and fourthly, great emotion to keep the mind and nerves stretched.

The mantrams of the East are, therefore, a very clever way to apply in practice all the four great rules of 'How to Get What You Want in Life', and would appear in any normal person as nothing more.

But, does this explanation apply to every case? Let me relate a true story to which thousands now living in India will testify.

Shri Narsiah was a humble stationmaster of the very unimportant railway station at Polreddipalayam on the Southern Railway in the state of Andhra Pradesh. But this humble and self-effacing man was the means of saving the lives of hundreds of persons bitten by poisonous snakes, including cobras, vipers and the deadly kraits. Should anyone be bitten by a poisonous snake anywhere in India, it was only necessary to send a telegram to Shri Narsiah at his station mentioning the name and address of the afflicted person. People in those parts are extremely poor and most can hardly afford to pay the cost of an express telegram. With this in mind, there is an unspoken understanding in the minds of the telegraphists throughout the region. When such a message is handed in, everyone handling the message, as well as the telegraphists receiving it, gives the message priority over every other telegram, even 'express' messages, however important they maybe. So we could expect Shri Narsiah to receive the telegram in a reasonably short time. Nevertheless, so terribly fast does the bite of a cobra work that the patient would be near to death anyway.

Growing to one side of the single platform at Polreddipalayam railway station is quite a short tree. It is a very peculiar tree indeed, different from all others. For it is a sacred tree and is the means by which the cobra's victim, perhaps a thousand miles away, can be saved from death. This little tree is festooned with small pieces of white rag, tied to every conceivable part of it within reach. Those little pieces of white cloth are torn from corners of Shri Narsiah's *dhoties*, or ankle-length *loinclothes*, for the stationmaster does not wear trousers of the ordinary western style. He is a high-caste

Brahmin and bears caste-marks upon his forehead. The climate is hot and he is barebodied invariably but his *loincloth*, wound tightly around his waist and extending to his ankles is his stock-in-trade for curing snakebites wherever they may occur.

Each time Shri Narsiah receives a snakebite telegram, he hastens to the little sacred tree, tears a strip of about six to eight inches from the bottom corner of his *dhoti*, ties it to a branch of the tree and mutters a secret mantra half aloud. The snake, provided it has not already been killed, is said to die at this instant. Narsiah then goes back to his work as stationmaster in the little cabin which is his office as if nothing untoward has happened. Maybe a thousand miles away the patient, lying on the ground in a coma with saliva dripping from the corners of his mouth, and with only a few moments more to live, suddenly opens his eyes, sits up and then stands erect. He has been completely cured!

Bear in mind that the victim was unconscious, at death's door. He certainly could not practise hypnotism not could he be hypnotised. Nor could he indulge in autosuggestion, not even in prayer. He could not do anything, for that matter, to help himself.

In distant Polreddpalayam, Shri Narsiah, interrupted in his duties, certainly did not waste time on any such practices. He had simply hurried to the tree, torn a strip from the lower end of his *dhoti* and uttered a mantra while he tied that strip to the tree. Then he returned to his duties. And the patient recovered!

If you were to ask Shri Narsiah how it was done, I do not think he will tell you.

At one time of my life I worked in the Telegraph Department for nearly thirteen years, and I transmitted many such messages to Shri Narsiah. To satisfy my curiosity, I have subsequently telegraphed the snake's victim at the address given on the distress message. In every single case the man had been cured! What is more to the point, I was bitten by a cobra myself and a telegram was sent to Shri Narsiah on my behalf.

I had just returned from duty. The time was about 3 p.m. A hue and cry was suddenly raised by one of our tenants. 'Snake!' She screamed. Then, as she saw the spectacled hood, 'Cobra! Cobra!'

I had been catching snakes since I was eight years old and so thought nothing of it. Without difficulty I secured the cobra by grabbing its tail, while I put a stick across the back of its head. Quickly releasing the tail, I transferred my grip to the back of the cobra's neck. Then I lifted it up. The snake was completely helpless. I carried it to the box I generally keep ready for such eventualities and was in the act of throwing it in when the snake wound the free end of its tail around my other arm. It was quite a long specimen for a cobra. A female, if I remember correctly.

As the snake restricted my movements I was unable to open the lid of the box, so I called my servant-boy (known as a 'chokra') to remove the tail that was coiled around my arm.

The chokra started to do so timidly when the cobra transferred its tail-coils to the boy's wrist. He panicked. he gave a violent jerk to free his wrist and in doing so wrenched the head of the cobra from between my fingers. That reptile was fast, and before I could act, it had buried its fangs in the ball of my thumb.

I threw the wretched cobra into the box, closed the lid, and as I did not have too much faith in mantrams and stationmasters, hastened in my car to the local hospital for an antivenine injection.

But my people at home had firm faith in Shri Narsiah, and as the telegraph office was but two furlongs distant, the telegram to him was on its way before I reached the hospital.

There was considerable confusion when I told the nurse at the emergency section what had happened. She said I must see the duty doctor and went in search of him. The doctor came back with her and asked what had happened. I told him. He asked whether I was certain it was a snake. Finally, he went in search of the serum.

He came back looking rather bothered. Apparently the hospital had run out of stock. He told me to hurry to another hospital which was over two miles away. I was feeling giddy by now with a pain in my thumb and hand. I got into the car and made for the other hospital, where I was given 10 cc of antivenine serum intravenously.

But my people had sent a reply-paid telegram to Shri Narsiah and to this he had replied, 'Don't worry. Patient cured. Snake dead.' The hospital detained me for about four hours to see how I fared. Except for severe urticaria set up through serum reaction, I felt more or less none the worse for my experience. The giddiness had passed and there was no pain in the region of the bite.

Finally I returned home and was handed Narsiah's reply. I read it and went directly for the box where I had put the cobra. I opened the box. The snake inside was quite dead. Not only dead, coiled up inside as rigid and stiff as if it had been made of metal.

How and why did that cobra die? It had not been injured by me or by anyone else. Also, it takes at least twenty-four hours for a dead snake to become so rigid. In this case only four hours had passed, yet the cobra had become so rigid that I could not uncoil it again, although I tried.

Not a very good case, it may be said, because I had been given the injection after the telegram had been sent. I should have waited for the stationmaster to act. But who would have done so in the circumstances? In any case, why did the cobra die? Why did it stiffen so soon?

Almost everyone who has lived in India for any length of time will be able to tell you instances of black magic. They abound in every corner of the land.

Sammy Soanes was a friend of mine. He had originally come from Goa then a Portuguese possession, and had bought a small property and settled down in Bangalore. A gentleman from Malabar bought the neighbouring house and moved in with quite a large household. Quarrels started between Sammy's people and the neighbours. My friend was of a quiet, non-interfering disposition, but these quarrels reached a pitch when he was compelled to make a police report as well as take legal proceedings.

Now his neighbour, the man from Malabar, although a recent-comer, had already become notorious as a black magician. He called Sammy to the stone wall that separated their respective properties and told him flatly that if he did not withdraw both cases against him forthwith, he (the neighbour) would make Sammy bedridden for life.

Sammy laughed at him. The man from Malabar turned on his heels and walked away.

As I have said, Sammy was a good-tempered soul. He forgot about the incident in a couple of hours and that night went to bed at his usual early hour. But he could not rise early the following morning. He could not get out of bed at all, for he was unable to raise himself. He was paralysed from the waist downwards.

Panic seized him as he remembered the happenings of the previous day. Mrs Soanes, who had overheard the neighbour's threats, pleaded with her husband to allow her to carry his abject apologies to the man from Malabar. Perhaps he would be merciful and forgive. Then Sammy would be able to get out of bed once more.

There is a strange quality that docile persons possess. You can drive them just so far, but suddenly they will reach a point when they can be driven no further. The neighbour's threats had reached that point. Sammy refused to apologise. Instead, he urgently summoned a Nambodripad, also from the West Coast of India, who was a personal friend and had settled down in Bangalore a couple of years earlier.

Krishnan, Sammy's friend, duly answered the summons and declared at once that the neighbour was responsible for Sammy's paralysis. He said, after some further consideration, that the magic used to bring about Sammy's incapacity was the work of a powerful 'yaksha'. So powerful, indeed, that his own familiar was not strong enough to undo it and put Sammy upon his feet again. What he could do, however, was to bring a similar spell to bear upon the neighbour, so that he would become paralysed himself and confined to his bed in turn.

Sammy gave the green signal to this and by the same evening the man next door suddenly lost his power to stand upright and within the hour found that he, in turn, could not move from the waist downwards. This led to a sort of contest in casting spells between this nasty neighbour and Sammy's Nambodripad friend, working on behalf of Sammy, in which the latter very definitely came off much the worse. Sammy was stricken with high fever, was unable to eat or drink, and the paralytic stroke that had afflicted him showed no signs of abating. He had to be fed intravenously. The neighbour, on the other hand, had managed to overcome the Nambodripad's spell and was back on his feet again.

It was at this stage that Mrs Soanes, unknown to her husband, visited the black magician next door to beg his pardon. When he opened the door to let her in, he remarked 'I knew you would come. It was just a matter of time.'

This man was a haughty fellow and spurned her apologies for a long time. Finally he agreed to remove the spell and restore Sammy to health in return for a sum of five hundred rupees, the full amount be paid in cash and in advance.

Mrs Soanes never doubted for a moment that he would keep to his terms. But where was she to lay hands on five hundred rupees without her husband's knowledge? Then she remembered the heavy gold chain lying at the bottom of her steel trunk. That and two gold bracelets she had bought after years and years of hard labour and saving.

She took the article to Borilal, the local moneylender. They were worth over two thousand rupees, but after much pleading and begging, that skinflint agreed to give her six hundred rupees in loan, although he did not actually present her with this amount in cash. Rather, he deducted the full interest for one month which he claimed came to just one hundred rupees, in advance, and gave the balance of five hundred rupees to his client.

Mrs Soanes hastened to her neighbour's house and timidly knocked at his door. After a while the black magician answered her summons. He nodded perfunctorily and allowed her to enter. Gruffly he commanded, 'Give me the money.'

Meekly, Mrs Soanes handed over five hundred rupees in notes. The man counted the money. Then he rudely dismissed her, saying, 'You may go. Your husband will be able to stand by this evening.'

Mrs Soanes did not dare to ask any questions, but almost fled from that awful presence. As the sun set that evening, Sammy suddenly told his wife that he felt well again, and to substantiate his words he scrambled to his feet. Mrs Soanes never told him about her chain and bracelets. She was too poor to redeem the articles, so she had to fake a burglary and say they had been stolen. Sammy believed her.

This story is true. I knew Sammy Soanes personally for years and visited him when he was paralysed. At that time he told me about the spell cast by his neighbour, and his own friend's (the Nambodripad's) unsuccessful efforts to free him. Mrs Soanes told me the rest in confidence, later on.

I do not wish to repeat myself, but there is a case of my own which I have related in an earlier book. A person who knew this art took a dislike for me. As a result I was awakened around 3 a.m. for several days with a feeling of being choked by a heavy weight upon my chest. I also heard measured footsteps outside my window, but there was never anybody there. Upon a whim, I consulted a local magician, who is very famous in my home town. Before I could speak, he told me the exact purpose of my visit. He also told me to go home, measure a certain distance from my window and dig down into the earth a certain depth. I was to destroy what I found there, whereupon I would be left in peace.

I measured out the stated distance, dug down the required depth, and found a small effigy with hair fastened to it. That hair looked remarkably like my own. I destroyed the effigy and was never troubled again.

I could relate many more tales of this sort, but they would become boring. It is sufficient to impress the fact that the people of India and especially those in the south of this peninsula, are brought up with black magic as an acknowledged fact from their earliest days. Nobody would ever think to question or doubt the reality; black magic is so involved in everyday life in this land that hardly any adult male of any community, other than westerners—who are considered not to believe in anything anyway—will go out alone after nine or ten o' clock at night until about five o'clock in the morning, by which hour evil spirits are considered to have gone to rest.

To carry pork, raw or cooked, after sunset is to invite being struck down by an evil entity. This is more so if you happen to be walking barefoot. It is safe, however, to carry pork provided you also carry a piece of charcoal. The devil will then leave you alone.

Members of certain tribes and communities are accredited with being steeped in magic from their childhood and the average Indian will avoid having anything to do with such a person, as if he had the plague. Three of these communities (actually they are part of particular tribes of aborigines who have been in the land from the beginning of time so to speak) come to my mind. They all speak the Telugu dialect and belong to what is now the state of Andhra Pradesh, located in the centre of southern India. These tribes are the Theyli Marajas, who speak Urdu as well, the Koya Mamas, and the Dawa-Lokey (Dawa means medicine and 'Lokey' means people. Hence 'people who give medicine', literally 'medicine men').

All three of these tribes have woven a strong superstition around themselves in the course of generations. When they walk down a village street, children run inside and adults close and fasten their doors. All of them live as mendicants, but they are mendicants with a difference. These people do not beg humbly for food, clothing and money. They demand these things and present their demands under open threat of reprisals if they are not met, so that few dare to deny them.

The Theyli Marajas dress in loose *jabbars* (kneelength shirts), covering *dhoties* wrapped around each leg individually, and wear turbans ending in a decorative fan above their heads, with the other end hanging down their backs. Falling over the shirt, both back and front, is a sort of apron reaching from shoulder to ankles. They carry small, two-stringed violins, consisting of a tin or box body with a bamboo extension, the tin or box employed being gaily decorated with cowrie shells. There is no bow to this instrument and no attempt is made to play it. Apparently it is not intended to produce music, but rather to announce the arrival of its owner, who plucks the strings with his fingernails. The resultant 'ting-ting' announces that a Theyli Maraja has come, and people hastily get something ready to give him in the way of grain or money to induce him to depart as quickly as possible.

These people are professional palmists, and in return for the gifts they receive will tell fortunes with surprising accuracy. So clever are they, in fact, that most people would rather not have their fortunes told for fear of hearing of coming sickness or early death. Rather they present their gifts hastily and invite the wandering Maraja to be on his way.

The Koya Mamas are a tall, very dark tribe of mostly lean men with coal-black, piercing eyes. They wear long hair, rolled up in a coil upon their heads and decorated with peacocks' feathers or a long-toothed comb. Invariably bare-bodied, with strings of gaily-coloured glass beads, they wear a long, tightly-fitting *dhoti* in the manner of a skirt. Another division of this tribe hails from the wilder parts of the country. Its representatives wear little or no clothing, except for a short *loincloth*. These people decorate their arms with amulets and bracelets made from the roots of trees or carved from bone, wear necklaces made from the coloured seeds of wild plants and trees. As beggars they are very demanding and have the knack of rubbing the base of the palms of both hands together when soliciting alms, while rapidly announcing: 'Look, it's coming soon ... See, it's on its way ... Soon, now. Very very soon it will be here ... Ah, I can see it now; there just there. Oh there, come, come this way.'

The people from whom they are begging, when they hear these words, attach great significance to what, or whom, the 'It' mentioned by the Koya Mama might be, and hastily force a gift upon him, inviting him to go and visit the neighbour next door.

The Koya Mamas have a further knack of introducing a strand of horse hair between the heels of their palms when they rub them together. A tiny charm is attached to this hair; after vigorous rubbing the strand seeks to unravel itself, thus causing the little charm literally to dance on the Koya Mama's palm. If you give him a rupee, he will present you with this charm (minus the horsehair of course) as a very lucky keepsake.

The Dawa Lokey generally send their womenfolk out to beg, even this task being considered beneath their menfolk, apart from being too strenuous. These women wear no jackets, but move from house to house barebreasted and dressed in single-coloured cotton sarees. Their 'doctor's bag' consists of a quilted cloth with the four corners meeting together over a short stick, which they carry across their shoulders in the manner of a gun. Inside the cloth is an assortment of roots, herbs and powders in small boxes. This forms their pharmacopoeia. There is no illness for which they have no cure, and they will try to impress one by answering in a different language from the one by which they are addressed. Should one happen to be conversant with this second language and answer in that dialect, the medicine-woman will then try third.

These itinerant doctresses announce their arrival at your front door in peculiar singsong voices with the words 'Dawa Lokey' repeated over and over again. Strictly speaking they are not beggars, as they earn their living by dispensing their herbal medicines. Depending upon the sagacity of the individual concerned, some of the roots and leave and powders they sell are singularly efficacious.

Every married couple in India desires to have children. This for two reasons. The first and most important because to be childless carries a great stigma on the wife as barren and incapable of bearing offspring. Very few people stop to consider that it might be the man who is to blame, and not the woman, for it is at once taken for granted that the woman is barren, and barrenness in India is a terrible affliction. It is thought that the gods are unfavourably disposed to such a woman; maybe she is immoral and has lost the capacity to bear offspring, or maybe she is diseased. But whatever the reason the poor woman gets all the blame and she, not her husband, is looked down upon with a mixture of pity and contempt, and suffers too, from the attitude of superiority among her fertile neighbours.

The other reason for this fear of childlessness is, of course, the desire for the continuation of the family, and for this reason it is a son who is desired and not a daughter.

There is in India a vast difference between having a son and having a daughter, and if a man is lucky enough to be the father of a number of sons he is considered to be on top of the world. For each of the sons, at the time of marriage, brings in a dowry. This dowry generally takes the form of a couple of thousand rupees or more, jewellery, land, a house or lower down the scale a car, a radio-set or transistor, or maybe a pair of gold rings or an automatic gold watch.

If, on the other hand, the man is unfortunate enough to have a daughter for whom he has to find a husband, that man is at the other end of the stick. For it is he who will have to do all dowry-giving to the bridegroom, who gives nothing in return, and if that man is unfortunate enough to be the father of several daughters he is indeed undone, as he will have to part with as many dowries as he has daughters. Nor will he be able to dodge the issue by keeping his daughters unmarried. To have even one daughter unmarried carries with it a fearful disgrace, for everyone will say that she is a bad girl and not a virgin; hence nobody will marry her. To have a number of unmarried daughters is to reach the bottom in public esteem. No girl is allowed to marry until her elder sister is married before her. Hence, if the father is poor and cannot afford to pay the required dowries, none of his daughters can marry and they are all dubbed as prostitutes, for to the person in the street there is only one reason for any girl to remain unmarried. Otherwise, surely someone or the other would have come forward to marry her. The reason why nobody has done so must surely be that the girl, and very likely her whole family, are immoral. The question that the father might be too poor to pay the dowries is conveniently overlooked.

As a consequence of this custom, the parents of every boy try to get a wife for him who brings the highest dowry. Conversely, the parents of a girl must look for a boy whose parents, in their turn, are prepared to accept a dowry of as little as the girl's parents can afford. And it is all left to the parents of both sides to bargain and barter. The boy and girl have no say in the matter, or in the choosing of their mates.

Money, having become paramount in India, as indeed it has throughout the world, the outcome is that it is comparatively easy to get your boy married and correspondingly difficult to get your girl married. As in most other countries, the birthrate, or survival rate of female children in India exceeds that of males, so the situation grows more difficult as the years pass for those unfortunate people who consider themselves to be cursed with a family of daughters.

In the overall picture, as people do not want to be childless for the reason I have already mentioned, the work of the government and of family planning organisations is extremely difficult. The significance of the threatened 'population explosion' is entirely lost on the average Indian ryot and poor person.

Poverty today is so great, and the cost of living so high, that a married couple can never think of having any form of hobby or recreation, however simple. Nor can they furnish their houses or buy any of the good things of life, not to mention food. This hand-to-mouth existence creates a deadly routine. Both husband and wife can afford to partake only of a very frugal *nasta* (breakfast), consisting of a small rice cake and a sip of coffee. Then both go out to work. The midday meal is equally frugal, and when they return in the evening the wife has to cook dinner, which again is frugal enough and consists of only a little curry and rice. After that, the couple retire for the night. They do not read, as they are illiterate. Even if they could read, they are too poor to afford the electricity or the kerosene required to illuminate their tiny rooms, many of which are hardly better than hovels.

What is there, anyway, for them to lie and discuss? The scarcity of food? The rising cost of living? Life's problems, and more problems and yet more? The only recreation that remains to these poor people is sex. It costs nothing. Further it does bring with it a measure of forgetfulness, of satisfaction, and a certain joy. Thirdly, when both are bullied at work by grasping employers, who drive them all day for what they can get out of them in the form of labour all day in return for a miserable pay, the realm of sex is something in which the man, and more rarely the woman, can at least dare to boost their frustrated egos. They can really let themselves go without fear.

Now, into the midst of this picture, admittedly dismal, comes a group of people who preach that even this one remaining pleasure should be eschewed. They are the members of the Family Planning Centre, introduced by the government at the behest of the UNO (who are all foreigners anyway), and they say that a married couple should have no children, or at most two children, and not more. These people say that the world is too full of children, and soon will be too full of men and women, and there will not be enough food to go around. As if there was enough food even now! The way to avoid all this, say the Family Planning people, is for each man and woman to undergo an operation. Alternatively, the woman may wear a loop, or swallow a pill now and then, or use some other sort of device.

So the villagers ask themselves: what in the world is life coming to? Our fathers, our grandfathers, our great-grandfathers, all enjoyed sex! We enjoy sex! Now these people tell us these things. They are trying to take away from us the only pleasure that remains to us. We have nothing else to enjoy but the act of sex. Must we give that up, too? Because one day some years hence, the world will be too full of men and women and there will be no food to eat! Where will we be then? We are starving now anyway, and we may not live another five years. Maybe not even another one. Certainly not for twenty or thirty years? So leave us in peace to enjoy the one and only pleasure left. Mind your own business and leave us to mind ours. Why, only the other day when we went to the coffee shop for a sip, we heard all the people there laughing heartily. 'What is so funny?' Some of us asked, 'Let's share the joke.'

It was sometime before anyone could stop even to speak. At last one said, 'Remember the Family Planning doctor who used to lecture to us daily? And remember the nurse who fitted our women with loops, and distributed pills among them? Well, he has made her pregnant and now she is on maternity leave.'

'Ho! Ho! Ho! Ha! Ha! Ha! Her own loop must have fallen off!'

On the other hand, my friend 'Samiar' (a term of religious respect), who lives on a little hillock not far from my land near Pennagram, in Salem district, plies a more popular and a far more lucrative trade.

Just over five feet tall, little Samiar (who is getting on in years now) enhances his stature by wearing several coils of very dirty black false hair upon his head. He has brilliant, piercing black eyes and wears huge earrings. On ceremonial occasions he decorates his forehead with white and red caste marks. For the forty years or more that I have known him, Samiar's reputation as a medicine man who can make barren women bear children has not ceased to soar. Hundreds of women have been brought to him, and as many have come of their own accord.

Samiar charges a very low professional fee for this service; just ten rupees for a poor woman and a fifty for a very rich one. The other condition is that the woman must be left alone with him in his hut during the hours of daylight. (To make such a condition extend into the hours of darkness would be scandalous, would it not? But surely nothing could possibly happen while the sun was shining, and after all, he is a 'Samiar', is he not?) Not so strangely, about half of the women become pregnant, but what is more strange is that most of those who do become pregnant have husbands who are sickly or otherwise wanting.

As I have hinted, I know Samiar extremely well. What very few others know is that he is a powerful hypnotist; also a rascal of the first degree, although an extremely jolly and likeable rascal. What is strangest of all is that many of these children, as they grew older, become rascals too, but jolly and likeable ones, and all of them have brilliant piercing, black eyes.

I have wandered in this country all my life, in its jungles, in its villages. I have mixed with hundreds of its poorest folk and talked to them. What I have written is only what they have told me in their own words. Of course, I understand the threat of 'population explosion'. I know, and can and do appreciate what the Family Planning Units are trying to do. But I greatly fear it will not work. The poor Indian, like everybody else, is human even if he is poor. He wants something concrete for himself, here and now, and is scarcely interested in what happens in the future, even only twenty or thirty years hence. He does not expect to live that long himself. And he could not care less what happens to those alive at that time.

Since there is no alternative recreation for him, since the conditions of living will continue to be as hard and difficult, and will grow harder and more difficult from day to day, he (and she) are not going to give up or even curtail in any way the one and only recreation they have left to them—the pastime of 'sex'.

India is being flooded by young people of all nationalities who come to the country in the thousands every month. Except for Russians, we meet folk from the Americas and from western Europe, even from Japan, wandering about the streets of our cities and towns. Some are 'hippies' but the majority are not, although it will be difficult for you to find any in normal western dress. On the contrary, some adopt the saffron gown and heavy head necklaces of the Yogi, the short *loincloth* and bare body of the Indian labourer, the loose pants with outside shirt of the northern Indian, with hairstyles varying from long hair and heavy beard through all the intermediary stages to no hair at all on either head or face. Mostly they are to be seen with hair flowing wildly in the breeze and in other cases wound around the head in elaborate hairstyles. The women of these groups appear equally odd:

a few wear sarees draped around themselves rather clumsily and not in the graceful manner of an Indian woman, while others wear the 'kameez' and 'calva' (the shirt and tight trousers) of the northern Indian ladies. Some come in ultra-mini skirts, while a number are at the opposite extreme, wearing dresses of ankle-length that defy definition.

Curiosity has urged me to talk to a number of these visitors in an effort to understand them, and this much I have gleaned, that almost everyone has confessed that he or she has found no place in the world like India. Some of them have travelled widely, and all of them hope to spend the rest of their lives in India. I have then inquired what it is they have found so attractive, but to this question I found a great variety of answers. Some say this country is very peaceful, the people very nice, the climate excellently warm, the sunshine superb, food and living very cheap. Others say they have a great urge for matters spiritual which they cannot satisfy in their own country, where the rush and bustle is too great. All are agreed on one thing. Time counts for nothing in India; there is no hurry about anything and there is always a tomorrow.

A large number of these people have attached themselves to *ashrams* or to individual Yogis in different parts of this peninsula. One of the main centres is at Pondicherry where men and women of different races have joined the Sri Aurobindo Ashram with hopes of settling down in the inter-racial township of Auroville, already planned and now under construction. This township promises to be utopian in character, where people of all nations, colours and religions may live together in peace and harmony—the only township of its kind in Asia. Many others have joined the following of the reincarnated Sai Baba at Whitefield. They are happy in their search for peace of soul, peace of mind and peace of living.

But all of these visitors are apt to forget a very important factor; actually, the most important factor of the lot. They have money sent out to them from their home countries, and if it were not for these remittances they would not be able to live in India at all, whether in an *ashram* or elsewhere, for as visitors and foreigners they are not allowed to take up work and be paid for it. It would be well for them to bear this fact in mind always, and not to speak so bitterly against their own lands as some of them do. For I repeat, it is their own country that gives them the money on which they find they can live so happily in India. Should these remittances for any reason cease, these visitors would have to go back to their countries and the 'rat-race' from which they have fled. And they will have to go back in a terribly great hurry, for each day they delay would make them that much more hungry.

But we have another type of foreign visitor, one who appears to want to break all the laws of the host country and escape the consequences by virtue of the fact that he is a citizen of another land. I am certain these people would never think of behaving in their own lands as some of them do in India. No doubt the comparatively easy living, the lack of the time factor, the probability that they will get away with it nine times out of ten, if not ninety-nine times out of a hundred, tempts them to act in this way, not realising (or caring) that their action boomerangs upon themselves, and upon their own countrymen wanting to visit India, and lastly on unfortunate people like myself who have chosen to remain in India and make it our home. Because of such wayward behaviour, we are classed with them as undesirable, as pestilential white folk who have no business to remain in India, who should go back without further delay to wherever we, or our ancestors, come from. In the stress of situations created by thoughtless visitors, it is only natural for Indians to forget that some of us settlers whose families have been in this land for generations by virtue of our living and experience are as much Indian, if not more than they are themselves. We have helped to build India into what it is.

But let me return to matters more strictly Indian, from which I appear to have strayed. Rarely will an Indian of the working classes, man or woman, know his or her own age or date of birth. Little attention is paid to this event, although the anniversary of a death is always remembered. This is because a whole set of ceremonies has to be performed for the dead person, year after year on the anniversary of a death. No importance, however, rests on a birthday. This is not true, however, of the upper classes. Not only is the day of birth recorded but the exact time to the very minute. The reason is that each individual man and woman of the middle classes or above is required to have his or her horoscope cast. It is incumbent upon the parents to do this for their children, and astrologers, who earn a very comfortable living in India casting horoscopes, require to know exact details of time and place of birth to be able to cast the horoscope correctly.

The one thing that may be regarded as the curse of our country, and which the government from the time of Independence has tried, and is still trying hard to stamp out, albeit with little success, is the caste system. This system concerns only Hindus and not the other communities inhabiting this vast land. In simple words it means that every living Hindu, man, woman or child, must belong to one or other of the numerous castes that go to form the Hindu community. They belong to a caste, whichever it may be, by virtue of being born into it through parents of that same caste.

No person can change his or her caste under any circumstances. He can never promote himself to a higher caste whatever his merits or achievements. He is of that caste

118

because his parents belonged to it and his grand parents before them, and his great-grandparents before that, and so on. His caste is as unalterable as the laws of the universe. Some of these caste classifications are governed by the trade the individual follows. It goes without saying that his father, grandfather and so on, followed the same trade before him.

For example, scavengers or sweepers, as they are called, are at the lowest rung of the caste ladder. Cobblers, or 'clucklers' as these are termed, are a slight step higher, and so on till we come to the warrior caste and the highest of all, the priests or Brahmins.

To give you an idea of how the caste system operates, let me show you a true-to-life example. About fourteen miles south of my home-town of Bangalore is a wild and hilly area known as Bannerghatta, where I own a farmstead consisting of a furnished house, a stone-lined well, and five acres of land, which I purchased for less than Rs. 10,000 (about £556). Half a mile from this farmstead are two hamlets. The name of one is Sampigehalli, and the name of the other is Byrappanahalli. Each consists of less than 200 homes. About two-thirds of these buildings are brick-and-mud structures, and the remaining one-third are wattle-and-thatch huts. The population of each settlement is well within 1,000 souls. Nevertheless in each of these hamlets there are no less than seven castes. Among these, the Brahmins and Lingayats are the highest in status; then come the Vakalgiries, working down to Kurubas, Maloles, Waddars and Madigols.

The government has built wells in both places for the use of all the inhabitants. But do you think that anyone or everyone is allowed to draw water? Not a bit of it. The lower castes are strictly debarred. Incidentally, I myself am debarred from drawing water although I am not a Hindu and do not belong to any caste. The reason is that I eat beef. As a beefeater, I am considered as belonging to the lowest category of human being, lower even than a Madigol, if that were possible. Is not the cow a sacred animal? And I dare to eat it.

Then men, of course, never draw water. In a home such a task is considered to be beneath the status of a husband as master of the household. Only the women go to the village well. Yet, should a woman of one of the lower castes require water, she may go to the well with her pitcher, but that is all she can do. She must wait till a woman of a higher caste comes along; then she may ask this woman to be kind enough to draw a pot of water for her use. If the woman obliges, well and good. Should the woman be in too great a hurry and unable to spare the time, the low-caste woman must wait till some high-caste housewife, who can spare the time and is kind enough to oblige, draws the water for her.

One of the servants at my farmstead is named Ramiah. He is an old man and a Madigol. He lives with his son and daughter-in-law and two grandchildren in a wattle-and-thatch hut in Byrappanahalli hamlet. One night we had a great storm, with high winds and torrential rain. Ramiah's hut fell down about midnight. Do you think the family could shelter in one of their neighbour's huts or house? No! They were Madigols, that is of the lowest caste! So Ramiah, his son, daughter-in-law and grandchildren sat in the pouring rain all night amidst the remains of their fallen hut and continued to sit there till noon the following day, by which time the sun had partly dried both them and the thatch scattered upon the ground. Then they got together to rebuild what they could of their hut before nightfall. There was no alternative if they were to avoid sitting in the open for another night.

The hamlets of Sampigehalli and Byrappanahalli are still there and these customs continue to this day. The government has tried hard to eradicate them. But the customs are centuries old and, as everyone knows, old habits die hard. particularly does the caste habit, because everyone of a higher caste has such a glorious opportunity to exploit all the castes below him.

The government has also tried to help the tillers of the soil. It has given many of them a couple of acres of land per head, a plough and two head of cattle, along with a loan to build a hut for themselves. As often as not the recipients of these gifts sell the plough and the oxen within a month of receiving them, and try to sell or mortgage the land as well. That is going rather far, however, and nobody has sufficient nerve to conclude this last transaction by buying the land.

Ryots have been invited to take generous loans from banks on security of the title-deeds of their lands. The money is intended to develop the land for agricultural purposes by digging wells, fertilising fields and so on. The loans carry very low interest, are for ten years, and may be repaid in easy instalments. But the ten years come and go, and no instalments, easy or otherwise, are paid, nor interest. The lands are not fertilised or developed, nor are wells dug. The ryot has spent the money on his daughter's dowry and wedding or on himself, in having a good time. The lockers of the banks are filled with people's title-deeds and the banks are wondering what they are going to do with them.

Major organised crime is rare in India. Murders are frequent, but they are generally motivated by infidelity, jealousy or disputes over land. Suicides are common and people kill themselves for every conceivable reason. The folk are emotional and temperamental, and suicide follows in the wake of a normally simple everyday problem which might have been easily solved.

Far down in the crime scale are pocket-picking, petty cheating and pilfering. To the last two groups there is no limit;

it is taken for granted that your neighbour will cheat you should he get half a chance to do so and if you have not been clever enough to cheat him first.

By and large, the rich classes are very rich and the poor very poor. Between these two extremes is a vast middle class of people forming perhaps a third of the population. The very poor make up the remaining two-thirds, the rich people being but a tiny fraction of the whole population. These rich people—landlords, business tycoons, cinema stars and so forth—have little to do with the very poor and as a rule are not in the least considerate to them. The poor, comprising the bulk of the population, have been poor all their lives and for generations before, having descended from a long line of ancestors who have always been poor. Prior to independence in 1947, for hundreds of years they had been ruled and oppressed by foreigners as well as their own kith and kin in the form of maharajahs, chieftain, princes, zamindars, landlords and money-lenders. They think in terms of having had no past, a present that is extremely bad, and a future that is without hope.

With all this background of poverty, misery and general hopelessness, we should not be too hard on those petty faults and weaknesses which are but the natural outcome of generations of exploitation and overpowering sense of inferiority. It is to be hoped that the time will come when the races of India realise at last that they are an independent people and not just talk about it.

India is a beautiful land, inhabited by a nice, friendly people, more appreciated by foreigners than by themselves. The majority of Indians think in narrow terms of caste, religion and community rather than nationality. The rulers are doing what they can to correct them and create a sense of national unity, but they have an uphill task, with many ancient customs and prejudices to overcome—the chief of which is the caste system—and a host of self-interested people to beat. Old habits die hard, and in this instance it is particularly difficult to kill the old caste bogey for the very cogent reason that millions of persons classed as of high caste, live and benefit by it, as their ancestors did before them for untold generations. It is only natural that they are disinclined to relinquish a way of living that has been and still is of daily gain to themselves in every sphere—in their employment, their official, social and financial and domestic status—merely in order to satisfy an ideal of improving the country, when they know quite well they will not be nearly so well off should the caste system disappear.

Four

Some Indian Game Sanctuaries

I HAVE HAD THE PRIVILEGE OF VISITING FIVE OF THE GAME SANCTUARIES of northern India. These five, and a number of others, have been created by the government in a last minute attempt to save some of the noblest animals of the subcontinent from extinction. Among these creatures are the Asian lion that is found only in the Gir forest of Gujarat state, the one-horned rhinoceros that lives in the northeastern extremity of the country in the state of Assam and in Nepal, the Indian wild buffalo found roughly in the same localities as the one-horned rhino, and the swamp deer, sometimes called the *barasingha* (meaning 'twelve-horned deer'), because of the twelve tines that adorn this magnificent animal, six upon either antler.

I began a tour of five sanctuaries in the company of two American friends and a Canadian, and as I maintained a day-to-day record of all that happened, I had better present the facts as they occurred. As far as I was concerned, the journey started when I left the airport of Bangalore for Bombay on the morning of March 3, 1970. It was a smooth fast flight, with nothing much of interest to see. We flew over Belgaum and soon saw smoke rising from several forest fires that were raging on the ghats between Poona and Bombay.

In exactly one and a half hours we touched down at the Santa Cruz airport at Bombay, whence I went by taxi to the Nataraj Hotel, which was the arranged rendezvous with the other members of the party, whose plane, however, arrived only after a fifteen-hour delay.

Eventually we started one morning for the small airport of Keshod in Gujarat state, from which point air-passengers are conveyed to the heart of the Gir forest, where we had booked rooms in the spacious forest lodge, where travellers are generally accommodated. The plane—a Dakota magnificently dolled up and in excellent flying condition—carried us across the small strip of the Arabian Sea which separates the city of Bombay from the peninsula of Saurashtra, which forms the western portion of Gujarat state. We flew over several steamers and noticed shoals of dolphins leaping from the waves.

The airport of Keshod is a few miles inland. There we were met by the van that was to convey us to the settlement of Sasan Gir, fifty-five miles distant, in the heart of the forest of the lions. En route we passed the port of Veraval with its ancient Somnath temple. There is a legend here that when the Mohammedan invader, Mohammed of Ghazni, planned to destroy this edifice in 1026, two thousand Brahmins poured holy water, brought all the way from the Ganges river, upon the idols, and strewed flowers over them night and day, to win the grace of the Gods and avert disaster. Mohammed of Ghazni never destroyed the temple.

The road was dry and dusty and the forest, when we reached it, was equally dry, rather open, sprinkled with *babul*

125

trees and interspersed with dwarf teak and not too many thorns. Except for the teak, the scenery was reminiscent of Africa.

The 'Guest House', which is the grandiloquent name given to the forest lodge, was comfortably furnished and the *khansamma* (cook-butler-tableboy) laid out a welcoming meal. We found the officials of the Forestry department most obliging and cooperative.

What is popularly called the 'lion show' had been arranged for five o'clock that evening. A live buffalo-bait had been tied up about eight miles away and the pride of lions that had been located in the vicinity actually 'called' to the spot by the junior forest officials, corresponding in rank to the forest guards of southern India, but known in Gir as *shikarees* or *chowkidars*. Many of them are quite old, and have been in the employment of the Forestry department when the Gir forest belonged to Junagadh state and ruled by a Muslim prince. This prince flew to Pakistan when India annexed his territories, and that was how the Gir forest became part of the province of Saurashtra in the Indian state of Gujarat. The *shikarees* and *chowkidars* were transferred to service in the government of Gujarat, but many of them still proudly display the letters J. F. (for Junagadh Forests) in polished brass on their tunics.

Incidentally, no visitor is allowed to watch the actual killing of the buffalo-bait by lions. The authorities consider that this might encourage the taking of life. But there is no objection to watching the lions feeding once that bait has been killed by them. The bait costs the visitor Rs. 150, and there is also a fee for using still or cine cameras.

It is interesting to watch the *shikarees* and *chowkidars* actually calling the wild lions. There are generally two of these men present, and they make a 'Khik! Khik! Khik!' sound with their mouths, followed by a 'Kroo! Kroo! Kroo!' noise with their lips. The wild lions appear to respond to these calls, if they do not recognize the persons who are making them and actually approach quite close to the caller.

To be on the safe side, the guards are armed with single-barrelled guns of .12 bore, loaded with buckshot. I examined the weapons carried by the men who had called the lions and found them to be as ancient as the men themselves assuredly hailing from the days of the old Junagadh forests. I then questioned the men as to why they carried these weapons, and the older of the two replied that sometimes, although very rarely, a young lion in his prime would resent the presence of onlookers in numbers, armed with cameras big and small, who keep moving around while he and the other members of the pride are eating. This animal then becomes aggressive, begins to growl and excites the rest of the pride. Then anything might happen.

'I have been dealing with lions since I was a boy, *sahib,*' he confided in Hindustani, 'and my father before me, and his father, and his father before that. Always watch the tail, *sahib,* then the eyes. And listen to any noise the animal might make. When the tail begins to twitch and rise above his back, when those large green eyes lose their roundness and start to half-close, when the whining sound he is making—or perhaps he is making no sound at all, or maybe he is just grunting—changes to a rumbling growl, he is about to charge you. Run for your life then, if you think you can. Actually it will be useless, for you won't run very far. Should none of these things happen, you are safe, although it might only be for the moment. Never can you tell when these *shaitan log* (devil people) suddenly become angry. You should always watch, watch, watch. The tail *sahib,* and those big green eyes!'

Apparently the purpose of the ancient gun and its load of buckshot was to fire in the air if necessity arose, rather than at the offending animal should it begin to evince signs of rising excitement. My informer said that the noise of the shot invariably had the effect of calming it down. Personally, I think the main purpose of the old guns was to boost the courage of those who carried them.

There was a pride of six lions on the kill when we arrived shortly after five o'clock. It consisted of two full-grown lionesses and four half-grown cubs, two cubs belonging apparently to each lioness. Unlike tigers and most other animals, all the lions seemed to be on friendly terms with each other and there were no signs of quarrelling.

As we grew bolder, we went closer and closer, till we were within thirty feet of the feasting animals. My friends, who were equipped with cameras, were taking photographs as fast as they were able. At one stage one of the lionesses, possibly disgusted at our close presence, seized the kill by a hind leg and pulled so hard at it as to break the tethering rope. She started to drag the dead buffalo away.

Then an amazing thing happened. The two *chowkidars* ran forward, caught hold of the dead animal by a foreleg, and started to pull in the opposite direction. It was an incredible spectacle. A tug of war between two human beings and a wild lioness, with five other lions looking on and a crowd of human spectators. I would never have believed it had anyone told me. The foresters were no match for the lioness, who started dragging them along with the kill. Then, amazingly, they let go of the leg they were pulling and ran forward towards the lioness, shouting in unison at the pitch of their lungs. The lioness released her hold, leaped backwards, and stood erect to look at the two men wistfully.

The other five lions were watching the scene with interest. We continued to regard it with amazement. Hastily, and not without considerable effort, the two men dragged the bait back to the tree to which it had been secured, and re-tethered it. I then lost my regard for the ferocity of the lions of Gir. As if nothing whatsoever had happened, all the lions returned to their meal, and in less than an hour there was not much left of the buffalo but bones.

The cubs, now replete with meat, began to take an interest in us. Their mothers, also full, rolled on to their sides and went to sleep. The sun was low in the western horizon.

Seeing themselves free of parental interference for once, two of the youngsters bounded playfully towards us, making guttural, mewing noises. Clearly they were purring as lion cubs usually do.

'Get back, *sahib*! Get back!' cautioned the elder *chowkidar* in a low voice, at the same time motioning urgently with his hand for us to retreat. Rather surprised at his unexpected concern at the approach of the cubs we nevertheless obeyed.

'If the mother wakes up and sees them near you,' he said by way of explanation, 'she will think you are going to harm them. Then all hell will break loose. You will come to know what the *shaitan log* are really like.'

Very soon the two lionesses awoke and returned to the remains of the kill which, as I have said, now consisted mainly of bones. One of the spectators, a professional photographer from Austria, got the *chowkidars* to drive the lionesses back for a moment while he hung a microphone from a branch of the tree beneath which the bones lay. Then he photographed the lionesses teasing the bones while he tape recorded the sounds.

Just about this time one of the lionesses had a small fracas with a cub that was worrying her. The Austrian recorded this too. Then he played the tape back. It was amusing to observe the expressions on the lion's faces when they heard their own growl and snarls.

Suddenly the pride stopped feeding. With one accord all heads, including those of the cubs, were turned away towards a *nullah* a few yards distant. We could see nothing. We heard nothing. The next moment, silently, from between the stems of teak and *babul*, a magnificent lion in his prime stepped forth, his mane was only slightly less heavy than that of his African cousin. Even at this distance and in the fading light, we could see the tufts of hair protruding from the elbows of his forelegs.

Our *chowkidars* became perturbed. They backed away from the pride and motioned to us to follow. We did so, retreating the fifty yards to where the van awaited us. We got inside.

'It is the bad lion, *sahib*,' said the older forester. 'When he turns up, the lion show must come to an end at once. For he brooks no spectators and is no respector of cars or persons. See even the other lions fear him.'

We turned to see the pride of six scatter in all directions. There came a thundering growl as the newcomer walked up to the bones, sniffed at them, and raised his head to regard us balefully.

The light was bad, but the photographers in the party wanted to stay to photograph the lion. The two *chowkidars*, however, were obdurate. To remain would be to court trouble, if not tragedy. They urged the driver to start the vehicle and drive away. When we complained the older man replied, '*Sahib*, we are responsible for the safety of all of you. That animal is a *shaitan* personified. If he had made up his mind to charge, these ancient weapons we carry would not stop him. Allah himself knows whether the cartridges would go off, for they are very old. We give him a wide berth when he appears. So also do the other lions, as you can see for yourself.'

It was dusk when we left the bad lion in undisputed control of the situation and began the return journey. We passed a few spotted deer, some late peafowl and a four-horned antelope a mile or so further and then, just as it was getting too dark to see, we heard a lion roaring a few paces from the track.

The elder *chowkidar* motioned to the driver of the van to stop, then banged the metal door with his hand while making the 'Khik-Khik!' sound with his mouth and the 'Kroo-Kroo!' noise with his lips. Within a few minutes a half-grown lion stepped out of the gloom, halted and gazed at the van expectantly. Clearly, he was hoping for something to eat in the way of live bait. We watched him for some minutes, then stepped out of the vehicle, whereupon the lion melted away into the shadows.

More excitement awaited us upon our return to the Guest House. Not content with the lion show, the enterprising Range Officer in charge had laid on a panther show as well. After dinner we were invited to attend this exhibition by following a pathway which led from the bungalow through scrub-jungle to a spot scarcely 300 yards away. A goat had been tied up to a post earlier in the evening and killed by a panther which was, apparently, a regular visitor to the spot, as he got an easy meal almost every second day in order to allow visitors to watch him eat. As with the buffalo-bait and the lions, spectators were not permitted to see the actual killing but there was apparently no harm in watching the panther eat once it had killed the goat. Incidentally, that goat cost us about Rs. 60.

All was ready. The panther had killed the goat—a black one—earlier, and then been driven off, being held at bay by a *chowkidar* with a big stick, squatting beside the dead goat. As darkness had fallen already, the scene was faintly illumined by concealed floodlights. The *path* we followed led into a big, circular iron-barred cage similar to what one sees at a circus but with this difference. At the circus the animals are in the cage and the spectators outside. Here, we were in the cage and the panther, outside.

Once we had assembled, the *chowkidar* with the big stick who had been keeping the panther off the kill, left his post, bringing his stick with him, and entered the iron cage with us. Then he secured the door behind him.

The panther had been watching and waiting for this moment. Obviously he was well practised in the procedure and may often have wondered to himself what it was all about. Perhaps he was wiser and wondered how stupid human beings were to go to all this trouble just to watch him eat.

Up he trotted within a few moments and fell with gusto upon the goat. The floodlights were gradually increased in intensity until, in about ten minutes, the scene was brightly lit. The panther became aware of this and must have felt uncomfortable, for he made one or two attempts to drag the goat away. But the tethering rope held fast, and the panther eventually resigned himself to tucking-in to meal under brilliant floodlight.

What might have been a rather unexciting exhibition was fortunately ended by the unexpected arrival of a hyaena. Perhaps this animal thought that he should also be given an opportunity to show himself. He sneaked up from behind, but the panther discovered him. With a snarl the panther left the kill to chase the hyaena away. The hyaena bolted, with the panther behind him, and the lights were dimmed.

Soon the panther returned, and a little later the hyaena too. Another loud snarl and another chase. Back came the panther followed by the hyaena who, growing bolder, showed himself. This time there was much snarling and growling on the part of the panther, and shrieking by the hyaena, but they never came to actual grips. Clearly the panther was not going to have everything his own way.

In the meantime the *chowkidar*, a young man this time, who had been through it all many times before and was manifestly bored, remembered that he had a young wife at home and felt that she would be in need of him. He coughed vigorously and clapped his hands. At the same time the flood-lights were put out.

The panther show had come to its end. In the darkness we could scarcely find the exit from the iron cage, but eventually we got back to the luxurious forest lodge and the foam-rubber mattresses and pillows on its beds.

At midnight I went out on the verandah. My companions were sound asleep. In the distance a lion roared. From the low hills on the opposite side came a chorus of roars in answer: 'Aaauuungh! Aaauuungh! Aauungh! Aauungh! Aungh! Aungh! Aungh! Aung! Aung!' The bewitching sounds died away into silence. I wondered if the 'bad' lion was calling to the frightened pride.

Before six o'clock the following morning we were on our way in the van to a jungle lake half-a-dozen miles away and reached it in time to glimpse a lovely sunrise over the jungle-clad hills to the east. The morning was pleasantly chilly in spite of the fact that we were in midsummer and in one of the arid areas of India.

A spotted stag brayed his challenge by the lakeside and in a few moments we saw him break cover and approach the water to drink, a dark silhouette against the golden *path* laid by the rays of the risen sun across the limpid water. A bevy of peafowl, quite twenty birds in all, followed one another to within a hundred yards of where the spotted stag was still drinking, and at that moment a magical sound rent the air.

133

A lion roared in a low valley beyond the roadside and another answered from a short distance further off.

A sambar-stag, hearing those roars, belled his alarm from a distant hill-top. I was excited, perhaps even more than my three friends from overseas. For I am familiar with the habits of tigers which are quite different from those of lions, and the calls of the lions enthralled me. I tore down the hill in the direction of the sounds and my friends followed closely behind.

Soon we arrived at a sandy stream. Impressed freshly upon the soft earth of the further bank were huge pug-marks. And they had not been made by a tiger—for there are no tigers in the Gir forest. They were the pug-marks of a lion.

We hastened onwards and were in time to catch a glimpse of the animal leap into the undergrowth and vanish. Clearly it had known that we were strangers and not the *chowkidars* to whom it was undoubtedly accustomed. We could not see much of his mane in the few moments the lion gave us. It was probably a young animal; certainly not the 'bad' lion, which was just as well.

The sun had risen by the time we got back to the car. The road circumvented a hillside and we were able to look down upon a vast sheet of water. Floating upon it in several places were what appeared to be logs of wood, but which I recognised as crocodiles. Then we began the return journey, passing more spotted deer and peafowl on the way. Also a small sounder of wild pigs.

The jungle-track passed several hamlets occupied by Maldharis, the name given to a pastoral sect of people who live in this area and bring their cattle into the Gir forest for grazing. They are a colourful race. The men wear loosely-gathered jackets and voluminous trousers, a turban or head-band of coloured cloth, a metal necklace with large ornaments, sometimes bangles of bone, and inevitably carry wooden staves. The women dress rather like the Indian gypsies, with ample brightly-hued sarees, tight-fitting jackets that reveal wonderful figures no Western woman could hope to approach, necklaces, bangles, ear-rings of silver, beads and imitation ivory. They are most handsome. The children look like miniatures of their elders but are even more brightly clothed.

In days past there was an abundance of water and grass in the Gir jungle. Animals were plentiful too. The lions had their natural prey and were not much interested in eating the livestock owned by the Maldharis, a species of buffalo, large and with curved, looping horns, which the peasants were mostly able to protect successfully.

The Maldharis were poor but happy in the forest with their buffaloes, whose milk and milk products they sold to the local *sahukars* or moneylenders to whom they were in debt. But with the passing of the old Junagadh state came unexpected problems. More and more cattle from all over Saurashtra and Kutch were driven into the forest, their numbers estimated at about 48,000 a year, in addition to the 21,000 stock owned by the resident Maldharis, who inhabit 129 *nesses*, or hamlets, corresponding to the cattle *pattis* in the jungles of southern India. The Gir forest then became a vast cattle camp, which created an acute shortage of water and grazing, for which the Maldhari now has to travel a long distance. With the continuous increase in cattle came cattle diseases that spread to the wild fauna. The shortage of grazing also cut the wild fauna down in numbers, and so did the increase in promiscuous poaching.

All these changes affected the lions; they began to kill the cattle and buffaloes of the Maldharis in greater numbers. The Maldharis became poorer with the rising cost of living; they could not afford to purchase cottonseed and groundnut cake to feed their herds. Municipal taxes made the sale of their milk products difficult and they were denied the benefits extended by welfare schemes in the towns for the sale of butter and ghee for the reason that they were not urban folk.

In desperation the Maldharis, who were generally not able to procure firearms, began to poison the lions that killed their stock by poisoning the flesh of the cattle that had been killed. When the lions returned for a second meal, they ate the poison and died in agony.

This is the same sort of thing that has led to the almost complete extinction of tiger, panthers and even hyaenas in southern India. But the position is even worse in the Gir; for whereas tigers and panthers almost always hunt alone and are therefore poisoned one at a time, the Gir lions, like their African cousins, hunt and feed in prides and are thus poisoned in numbers. We were told that nine lions had been poisoned in this manner very recently. This was shocking news, considering the fact that the lions of Gir are the only representatives of their species in the whole of Asia.

The Gir itself has also been intruded upon by cultivation around its perimeter, so that the area now comprising this forest is but 1,300 square kilometers or 576 square miles in extent. A census of the lions remaining in this jungle, conducted in 1955 by measuring and counting footprints, indicated about 247 animals. The next census in 1968 showed only 177 lions, a decrease of about forty per cent. The fate of the Gir lion is, indeed, hanging by a thread.

A century ago, the forests of Gir covered three times the present area. Recent statistics reveal that sixty-three per cent of the land surrounding the Sanctuary is under cultivation. With the felling of the forest and advent of more and more cattle, together with the presence of poachers and the poisoning of kills, the noble lion of Gir seems doomed to extinction.

The Sanctuary is now estimated to support a wildlife population of less than twenty-five per cent of its original strength, compelling the lions to rely almost solely on the buffaloes of the Maldharis for food. Their ability to get enough to eat is severely taxed. Although this animal is by nature a nocturnal hunter, existing conditions compel it to hunt by day because the Maldharis corral their stock at sundown.

The Maldhari settlements past which we drove in the van that morning proved to be small mud huts, thatched with sticks and leaves. Allowing a vacant space for the cattle, the whole area of each *ness* is enclosed by a strong, tall thorn fence, very reminiscent of the thorn *bomas* of African herdsmen, or in some instance by rock-and-mud walls. Indeed, the whole scenery in the forest is much like that of the thorny scrub-jungles of Africa except for the occasional stunted teak tree growing in between.

Should a lion succeed in jumping one of these fences or walls and killing a buffalo, his effort is vain, since he cannot get his kill over the obstruction to freedom. Should a lion succeed in killing one of the herd in the jungle, he generally loses most of the meat when the Maldhari herdsmen combine to drive him away to salvage the hide.

Incidentally, this also happens in southern India when the herdsmen drive a tiger or panther off the cow it has just killed. Occasionally the feline resents this intrusion and attacks a herdsman, mauling him, even occasionally killing him. That, in turn, has often led to the tiger or panther becoming a man-eater. I was told that the same thing has happened in Gir, although infrequently. Now and then a lion has taken to killing men and eating them; it has then had to be shot.

It is estimated that of the domestic stock killed within the Sanctuary fifty per cent are taken by lions and outside the

Sanctuary, up to eighty per cent. Panthers account for the remaining kills. As I have said before, there are no tigers in the area.

Because he is mostly deprived of his victim, either as soon as he kills or when he returns to the carcass to find the hide removed by the owners, the lion is of necessity compelled to kill more often than would be the case if he were allowed to gorge his fill. Statistics show that twenty-three per cent of the kills are not eaten at all, while the lions are barely able to consume ten kilograms of meat from a further twenty per cent of kills.

This cycle of unfortunate circumstances has brought the lions of Gir forest into conflict with the Maldharis who occupy the 129 *nesses* they have established all over the Sanctuary, as well as the owners of thousands of visiting cattle. Enraged herdsmen do not hesitate to shoot or poison such lions as they are able to if they will not be detected.

The government pays compensation to the owner whose animal has been killed by a lion outside the Sanctuary, but not when it has been killed within. This is not good enough. The Sanctuary, which was primarily created for the protection of these Asiatic lions, is not being allowed to function as it should and fulfil the purpose for which it was instituted.

Of the natural wild fauna three-quarters have disappeared. Most of the fertile valleys in the Sanctuary have been cultivated and a continuous strip of cultivation has already cut the Sanctuary almost in two. The felling of trees—mainly teak—continues, while the hordes of domestic livestock prevent saplings from replacing them. Nearly two million kilograms of grass fodder are removed from the Sanctuary every year. The Sanctuary has been reduced to an impoverished, artificial and heavily-exploited zone. The presence of the few remaining Asiatic lions alone has aroused worldwide interest, but only the government of India can save the situation at this last-minute stage.

I am glad to be able to record that the Central government has risen to the occasion and has entrusted the state government of Gujarat with a scheme called The Gir Lion Sanctuary Project, which started in January 1972. The Governor of Gujarat, Shri Shriman Narayan, envisaged a twofold target, the first object of which was to protect the lions of Gir in particular, as well as other wildlife, from poaching, poisoning and dangerous diseases. The second object is the socio-economic improvement of the Maldharis' condition.

Many meetings were held and resolutions passed, resulting in formal orders being issued by the government of Gujarat to: (1) Close the Sanctuary permanently to grazing by migrant cattle. (2) Enclose the whole area with an effective physical barrier. (3) Allot land outside the Sanctuary to the Maldharis at present inhabiting 129 *nesses* inside it, and to shift them, with their families and livestock, out of the Sanctuary in a phased programme. It remains to be seen how far these aims are carried out. One fact is certain. Should the programme fail to be executed, the Gir lion is doomed to extinction within the next decade. Any number of meetings and resolutions, stacks of orders that exist on paper, speeches by the highest officials, drawings, plans and schemes supported by statistical data will not save the lion. What is required is action, and that quickly.

It is discouraging to learn that, after the passage of a whole year, the Maldharis were still where they have always been, in their *nesses* within the Sanctuary.

After breakfast, at about ten o'clock, we left the forest lodge in the van to motor the dusty roads to the capital of the old Muslim ruler, a town named Junagadh, which is filled with ancient Muslim tombs and mosques. A quick lunch at the Circuit House and we were away again, this time bound for the royal palace of Wankaner, where we were to spend a night and day as guests of His Highness the Maharajah and the Prince Yuvaraj of Wankaner. The distance from Sassan Gir to the palace is 105 miles by road.

Petrol trouble delayed us, but we were more or less on schedule when we reached the palace at 5.30 p.m. where the Maharajah and the Prince greeted us with old-world courtesy, garlanding us to the particular delight of my friends.

Next morning the Prince took us out in a tourist cart to his father's private jungle of some 3,800 acres, situated about six miles away. The country consisted of low, rolling hills; the soil was very dry and clothed with dwarf *babul*. The Yuvarajah complained that the townspeople from Wankaner made inroads into his father's forest, cutting the sparse timber for firewood and poaching, if they got the chance.

We came to a palisaded house where the private salaried range officer and two forest guards in the employment of the Maharajah resided. These turned out and gave the Yuvarajah—and ourselves—a big salute.

Picking up one of the guards, we motored along the rough tracks winding around the hills and sometimes across them, if the ground permitted, meeting sixteen blue bulls, the colloquial name for Nilgai, in small batches, the largest consisting of five members, all male. We also disturbed two *chinkara*, a species of antelope smaller in size than blackbuck, a lone fox, and numerous sand grouse. The Yuvarajah told us that black partridge and sand grouse visited the area in large numbers during the monsoons, but went away with the approach of summer. The estate was covered with porcupine diggings and burrows.

The Yuvarajah invited us to stop over another day and motor with him to see the famous 'wild asses of Kutch.' These animals, of the donkey family but standing almost as high as mules, live in an area of this dry land somewhat over a hundred miles to the north of Wankaner. Unfortunately we were bound to a tight programme and just could not spare the time. Returning to the palace, we were struck by the large numbers of wild peafowl that strutted about and called to each other. Even the extensive grounds of the palace were full of them. Nobody shoots these beautiful birds in Gujarat. 'Pea-or! Pea-or!', their cries echoed from all around.

The Yuvarajah, who had appointed himself as our guide, took us next to his private farm, situated on the outskirts of the township of Wankaner, where we were shown around a lovely guest house that he was remodelling, with excellent furniture and, of all things, an up-to-date swimming pool, something unheard of in this arid land.

Close by was an ancient well, with steps of pure marble leading down to two terraces built into the sides of the well. From the centre of the well spouted a fountain of water that reached up to the higher terrace and then splashed down to cover everything, including part of the lower terrace, with a fine mist. We felt delightfully cool, as if we were standing on an air-conditioned verandah.

After lunch we left to motor to the capital city of Ahmedabad, 140 miles distant. I felt as if I were in another world, the countryside being totally different from that of southern India. It was a parched area, semi-desert, and this fact was emphasised by the strings of camels we passed on the road, their numbers sometimes assuming the proportions of a caravan. Seated on these animals were wild-looking men and women in curious array. Other camels carried their household effects, string-cots, all sizes of pots and pans, immense heaps of clothing tied into bundles, and miscellaneous other articles that could scarcely be identified. The afternoon was exceedingly hot. As we approached Ahmedabad, the country became slightly greener. It was evening when we reached our destination.

Part of our programme the following morning was to visit the Nal Sarovar lake, a bird sanctuary and a bird-watchers' paradise, but this had to be dropped. Due to two very severe summers in succession when the monsoons had failed, the lake had dried up completely. So we visited the local zoo instead, where we saw a large variety of animals and a collection of birds from all over the world that is really excellent. I was particularly interested in the snake-pit with its jet black cobras. No doubt owing to the colour of the local soil, which is very dark and known in these regions as 'black cotton-soil', nature has arranged that the creatures that live upon it should also be dark in colour to prevent them from being conspicuous, which would otherwise be the case.

Amidst a collection of tigers and panthers, and a pair of lions from Africa, were a Gir lion and two lionesses. This lion we discovered to be far fiercer than any of the wild lions we had met at Gir, even putting the 'bad lion' to shame. He repeatedly charged at his keeper and us, stopping only at the bars of his cage. Even the African lion was unfriendly. Assuredly, the big felines are far more docile in their wild condition.

That afternoon we took off by plane for the city of Udaipur, where we landed after a very bumpy flight of fifty-five minutes, due perhaps to flying over heated, almost desert land, barren, rocky and unfriendly to look down upon. From the airport we motored to the edge of a large and magnificent lake, boarded a motor-launch and chugged across to one of a series of islands that dotted the water. But this island was different from the rest, for upon it has been built a beautiful hotel, known as the Lake Palace Hotel, with sixty-five rooms that, for the most part, directly overlook the water. The building encloses an open-air garden, abounding with trees and flowering shrubs. It is the private property of the Maharana of Udaipur, till recently one of the important ruling princes of India. He has converted it into a tourist hotel and is running it himself.

In the evening we went by launch to visit one of the neighbouring islands, where the Maharana has a palace which is also being converted into a twenty-room guest house with a magnificent swimming pool. Some of the carving we saw in this palace were wonderful, being old Moghul and Rajput work of ancient origin. The Maharana has a huge palace on the mainland, too, and yet another on the top of a neighbouring hill. From where we stood, the hill-top palace seemed almost inaccessible, perched like an eagle's nest upon rocks at summit, it gleamed a pale pink in the rays of the setting sun.

The Prince also owns a number of shooting boxes scattered about the low scrub jungle of rolling hills that surrounds the lake. Around the city of Udaipur itself are the remains of a continuous wall, once built to protect it against the invading Muslim hordes of the great Moghul conquerors.

When the sun began to set behind the western hills and cast a rippling red-gold pathway across the waters of the lake, we heard raucous voices and saw a strange sight. Thousands upon thousands of green parakeets flocked across the lake from every direction to roost upon the huge trees that grew on the island. It is estimated that over 10,000 birds fly here to roost each evening, coming from areas over fifty miles distant. Each morning they fly back again to feed, but return punctually once more the following evening. This has been going on for centuries, as on the orders of successive Maharanas no one may molest the parakeets; this protection makes it possible for them to increase in numbers every year.

Packs of jackals could be heard that night, howling on the mainland: familiar and welcome sound, it brought back a hundred memories of nights spent in jungles, now far away in the south. The packs called and answered each other from shore to shore: 'Here! Here! Here! Heee-hah! Hee-yah! Hee-yah! Hee-yah! Yah! Yah!'

Then the following morning we took the launch for the shore, where a car conveyed us to the Maharana's main palace, a wonderful structure of white and black marble, with coloured glass windows, amazing carvings, and a rare collection of old armour and swords. Nearby was an ancient temple. And in the afternoon we set out for Jaisamal lake and game sanctuary, thirty-five miles away, passing through dry jungle in hilly country enroute.

In a little over an hour we arrived at the lake, an immense expanse of water. The Maharana has yet another two palaces here, on opposite shores. The lake appeared to be well-stocked with fish, and we could see them leaping out of the water and falling back again. The evening was bright and sunny.

We motored five miles into the heart of the adjacent, Jaisamal game Sanctuary to view a 'Panther show' of a different sort. The jungle was fairly heavy, but very dry. We passed two herds of spotted deer by the wayside, some of the stags carrying exceptionally fine heads. Our destination was an abandoned watchtower, constructed by a bygone Maharana and converted by his descendant into a shooting box. It was built of stone and was three floors high, and the walls were filled with loopholes presumably for firing through. It looked like a miniature fort, and overlooked a narrow, shelving valley, through the middle of which passed a dry streambed. On the further side of this valley was a gentle, sloping hillside. There were small glades clearly visible to us between the trees and low bushes.

About fifty yards beyond the shooting box a wooden platform, roughly five feet high, had been erected. It stood upon four legs and was a more or less permanent structure. The unfortunate goat, this time a brown one, was tethered on top of it and beneath was a trough, filled with water.

We were invited to enter the stone tower, where four cars were already parked, through a low doorway at its foot and to climb a narrow stairway to the third floor. There we found a full house of people assembled; they were seated in chairs before all the available loopholes that overlooked the platform and its goat. In this gathering were a film star and her friends. All of them were chattering, smoking, moving about and hailing each other in very audible voices.

It soon became clear that, so great was the audience, if we wanted to see anything we would have to go down to the floor below. This we did and chose four loopholes before any more people came along.

I could not resist the temptation of asking the agreeable Forest Range Officer (F.R.O.) in charge of the operations whether the authorities felt any harm was being done by allowing us to watch the panther kill the goat, telling him that in the Gir we had not been allowed to see either the lions kill the buffalo or the panther kill the goat prior to the 'show', as that was considered as encouraging the taking of life. The F. R. O. smiled disdainfully. 'We are Rajputs', he vouchsafed by way of explanation. 'Those fellows are Gujaratis.'

He then went up the stairway to where the film star and her friends were gathered, and soon the chattering ceased. He must have impressed on the party that this was no rehearsal.

Staring through the loophole, I glimpsed a single spotted doe across the dry stream in the mid-distance, soon followed by bevy of after bevy of peafowl. Then dark forms filtered through the undergrowth: a sounder of wild pigs. Then a slight movement behind a bush in the foreground caught my eye. I stared hard. A panther crouched close to the ground.

145

I had not seen him arrive. No one had. It was 6.15 p.m. The panther remained where he lay without moving. Obviously he was aware of people watching and preferred the greater darkness before he showed himself.

At 6.30 p.m. he moved slightly, but still did not risk an attack. It was seven o'clock and getting quite dark when the panther could contain its hunger no longer. From where it was crouching, the spotted cat leaped neatly on to the platform, walked calmly up to the goat that had turned around to face its attacker and was straining backwards at its leash, and almost unconcernedly seized it by the throat. The goat bleated once and kicked feebly. Then the feline pressed the head of its prey to the platform and held it there for a long time, till life was extinct.

It was getting more and more difficult for us to see anything in the increasing darkness when the Ranger pressed the switch that was to bring the spotlight into play, but there was no response. The current had failed.

We could barely see the panther tearing at the goat's throat to suck the blood from the jugular vein. A few minutes later it leaped down from the platform and drank deeply at the trough of water. Clearly this panther had been through the performance very often before and knew exactly what to do. Then it became too dark to see more.

The film star gave us a winning smile as she brushed ahead on the narrow stairway in the ground, and soon we were heading for Udaipur.

The next day was idle till the afternoon, when we left for the airport. We were bound for the distant city of Nagpur, from where we were scheduled to motor to the Kanha National Park. But there were many delays on the way, due partly to bad weather and partly to an argument at Delhi between the pilot and a passenger who turned up after the engines had been started, so it was not until early next morning that we landed at Nagpur. Rain was still falling.

But we had to be up again at seven o'clock to set off on a journey of 210 miles by car. Our entourage was of two vehicles: a car for travelling and a Land Rover for our use in the sanctuary, where some of the tracks, up and around steep hills, cannot be negotiated by an ordinary car. Meanwhile the Land Rover was hauling the trailer tightly packed with camping kit, a cook, a butler, a table-boy, and all manner of food for our use while we were 'in camp'. Also any number of bottles of Coca-Cola for my American friends. These stood upon ice in large ice-box, in rows like soldiers on parade. Nagpur is situated in Maharashtra state, while Kanha is in Madhya Pradesh. Thus we had to cross an interstate frontier and in doing so were required to sign a form. Our kit and foodstuffs were also examined with awe. It is not clear what the searchers were looking for, but what they saw must have puzzled them beyond belief. They passed us on without further argument.

Forty miles short of our destination the car became stuck in the mud. It had been raining heavily an hour or so earlier and the road was a morass. We got out to help and discovered we also had a flat tyre. To jack the car in that mud was a problem. There seemed nothing to do but wait for the Land Rover to catch us up.

Luckily it appeared fairly soon. We climbed aboard, changing places with the cook and the other two servants whom we transferred to the car. We left them to help the driver in his struggle in the mud.

The road was in a terrible condition due to the recent heavy rain and it was a difficult journey, even for the Land Rover, encumbered as it was with the heavy trailer behind. We passed through three forest *chowkies*, or checkposts, in succession, at each of which were displayed numerous notice boards with warnings against poaching and other offences. At every one of these a fee or tax of some sort was collected from us. At last we arrived at the guest houses, for there were quite a number of them.

When, as we unloaded the trailer, I saw all the food that had been provided for us, I was lost in amazement. How different was this fare from what I took on my own trips in the south! There, after the second day, my diet invariably consisted of dried *chappatti*, often without butter. Roast beef was the luxury, but only on the first day. Thereafter there were *chappatties* only, and of course lots of tea. Here we had turkey, duck, chicken, mutton, fish, fruits of every sort. Not one *chappatti* could I see anywhere, nor any sign of beef!

So we set off for the jungle in the Land Rover, a forest guard seated beside the driver to direct him. Within a furlong we met herd after herd of spotted deer, some of the stags carrying amazing horns. Grazing along with these animals, and sometimes by themselves, were herds of blackbuck. Now and again we could pick out the almost black form of a mature stag with its white belly, but for the most part the males were young. Does, along with their fawns, were quite numerous. Peafowl were plentiful, and we saw two red junglecocks. One flew across the track ahead of us while the other ran along the roadside for a while before dodging into cover.

The red jungle fowl of central and northern India is quite different from the silver-hackled bird of the south. Neither species changes its habitat: the central and northern bird is slightly smaller, dark in colour with rusty red wing feathers, and crows somewhat like a domestic cock. The southern bird is larger, with a silver-grey hackle, and wing feathers that look as if they have been painted with heavy oil-colours in a very dark brown border with dark spots. Feathers of the same kind adorn the hackle in addition to those of silver-grey. It has a very distinctive call: 'Wheew! Kuck! Ky'a! Ky'a! Khuckhm!' It is by far the more beautiful of the two varieties.

We returned to the guest house at sunset to find that the cook had performed a miracle and our supper was ready. The dining-room lay just off the verandah, so that while we ate we were able to listen to all the sounds of the jungle. Soon we heard a series of strange sounds, the like of which I had never heard before. Loud, trumpet-like cries, somewhat like the braying of a spotted stag, but with much more of the brassy resonance of a male sambar's note of alarm: 'Aa-hh-harmm! Aa-hh-harmm! Aa-hh-harmm! Aa-hh-harmm!'.

This was the call of a male *barasingha*! It is rather difficult to imitate that memorable sound on paper, but when you hear it, it is distinctive. And it is sad to think that in a few more years it will be heard no more. The barasingha, or twelve-horned deer, derives its name from its magnificent head of twelve tines, six upon either side, the word 'bara' signifying twelve in Hindi, Urdu and Hindustani. It is only very slightly smaller in size than a sambar, but is dark brown as distinct from the brownish grey of the sambar. Like the sambar, the stags have coarse, long hair on their flanks and around the neck and throat, where it almost resembles a mane. They are far larger than spotted deer.

Unfortunately, these creaturs seem to be rather silly, lacking the alertness of both sambar and spotted deer. They move slowly, heavily and sedately, and are slow to take alarm, slow to react, slow to run away. Nor can they run as fast as sambar, although the latter is bigger. The stags have the same habit as the nilgai or blue bull: they congregate in small herds of half-a-dozen without a single doe.

These characteristics have led to their downfall, inasmuch as they fall easy prey to the poacher, their principal enemy, in addition to marauding tigers and panthers, as well as wild dogs and even hyaenas. Barasingha, once plentiful in India, are now almost extinct. The Kanha Sanctuary, designed for their protection especially, holds but fifty-five of these beautiful animals. Kaziranga, and a few other sanctuaries, have rather more; but everywhere they are alarmingly scarce. Their future in India, together with the lion of Gir and the one-horned rhinoceros of Kaziranga in the northeast, is very bleak indeed.

I had not yet fallen asleep that night when I heard a tiger roaring. He must have been half a mile from the guest house. How good it was to hear that memorable sound again: 'Oo-oongh! Aa-oo-oongh! Aungh! Oo-oo-ongh!'.

We were away by six-thirty the next morning and very soon found the group of barasingha that had been calling the night before: five stags, all in a bunch together. Hardly a mile further on we encountered four doe barasingha, these also in a group by themselves. Not far from them we passed three groups of blackbuck and many herds of spotted deer, one of them comprising over a hundred animals. Bevy after bevy of peahens, and some isolated cock birds, scattered to right and left of us. It was a peaceful scene until we observed two jackals slinking through the grass close by, silent reminders of the sudden death that can overtake the creatures of the jungle at any moment.

Leaving the park-like country that is the abode of the deer, the Land Rover took us into the low hills that surrounded it. Soon we saw a pair of bison staring at us from under the tall *sal* trees. The jungles of Kanha are very different from those of southern India. Stately *sal* trees clothe the former, tall and straight and beautifully green. The absence of lantana undergrowth is noticeable, also of the 'wait-a-bit' or *Segai* thorn, both of which make wandering in the south very difficult at times. This, and the absence of wild tuskers, which are dangerous and a positive hazard for the unwary hunter or greenhorn naturalist on foot, make Kanha a paradise for 'ghooming', the Hindi name for wandering about. On the whole, I would say the Kanha jungles are about the best for this purpose that I have ever visited.

The next morning we drove through heavy forests, covering over thirty miles or so of rising, hilly country to a high ridge where the natural teak opened on to an extensive maidan or expanse of low grassland, entirely surrounded by the jungle.

We were agreeably surprised to be told that the government of India tourist department plans to convert this area into a landing-ground sufficiently large to operate a Dakota plane service from Nagpur for the convenience of foreign tourists and local sightseers, thus obviating the long car-journey of 210 miles from Nagpur.

This plateau overlooks a famous former shooting block, the Bandla Block, which still goes by the same name. Many old hunters who have spent their early years in Madhya Pradesh, which was previously known as the Central Provinces, will remember this area with nostalgic affection as one that produced some of the most magnificent tigers, for which these forests were world-renowned. On the return journey we encountered as many as seven sambar together, quite an exceptional number for creatures that generally graze in solitude; also many families of langur monkeys and any number of red jungle fowl, and the small barking-deer or muntjac. Returning to the low, and the country, we passed the usual families of spotted deer and blackbuck.

In the morning we were back again in the Land Rover, meeting once again large herds of spotted deer and blackbuck, any number of peafowl and a few barasingha. In desperation the authorities are now planning to enclose the barasingha within a high wire-fencing of fairly close mesh, covering an area of a few square miles, to protect them against their natural enemies, tiger, panther and wild dog, and of course poachers. It is to be hoped this succeeds, although by its adoption these animals could hardly hereafter be classed as living in a truly wild state. Still, I suppose that fifty barasingha within a fence are better than no fence and no barasingha!

By this time we were tired of driving about in the Land Rover. Three elephants, belonging to the forest department, were obtainable on hire, so we changed over to the backs of a couple of pachyderms and went searching the borders of some *nullahs* in the hopes of seeing a tiger or panther. But we saw only the usual barasingha and blackbuck.

At about four o'clock we took the Land Rover again to look for tigers, but we saw only spotted deer, peafowl, red jungle fowl and langur monkeys. A couple from New Zealand, who had booked elephants for that evening, were more lucky. They had gone separately on their respective mounts, and while Jack Doon, the husband, was returning he came across a spotted stag struggling on its back. A few yards distant crouched the panther that had attacked it, caught in the act of slinking away. The stag was evidently badly mauled and its spine had been broken. The elephant Jack was riding upon had only recently come to Kanha. A nervous female, it bolted twice upon seeing the stag and its assailant. When the mahout finally succeeded in controlling and bringing it back, Jack discovered the panther again and took pictures of it for nearly thirty minutes, during which time it climbed up a tree, jumped down again and then went up a low rock. Margaret Doon, while returning on the other elephant, came across a dead spotted fawn. For some reason its killer had abandoned the meal and now the fawn was being devoured by a pack of jackals.

That night an official who had arrived at the guest house insisted that we go out with him at nine o'clock and use his spotlight to try to see bison or a tiger. As a matter of fact, such journeys in vehicles with spotlights are strictly disallowed in Kanha, but being the boss himself, and for our sakes, he made an exception. We found a very large bull-bison, followed by a cow a few paces behind, but no tiger ; and when returning met the usual herds of spotted deer and blackbuck and, close to the bungalow, a couple of sambar.

At dawn the following morning the official took us out again, this time using our own Land Rover and driving it himself. We went to a natural salt lick, where a tower had been constructed, with a ladder reaching to a covered platform. This tower overlooked a large jungle pool in which the water was partly covered with beautiful pink-petalled lotus flowers. Within a few yards of this pool was the salt lick in a hollow in the ground. A sambar stag that had been at the salt lick thundered away at out approach, while from the pool came the flapping of a myriad wings and swarms of spot-bill and brahmini ducks arose, spiralling into the air with a whir of wings. As they flew round and round they uttered sharp cries of alarm.

We also disturbed other creatures: a herd of about fifteen adult bison with half-a-dozen calves, all of them led by a huge master-bull. They had been drinking at a smaller pond opposite the watchtower and we had not seen them at first. This pond was to the west of the track we were motoring down, and in the park-like section of the country, while the watchtower and the lake and salt lick, surrounded by forest, were to the east. Thus the track formed a sort of natural boundary between the two types of country. The master-bull, with his following, saw us and attempted to cross the track to get back into the forest. We prevented them from doing this by racing the Land Rover ahead, or in reverse when the need justified it, so that the bison always found our vehicle between them and the jungle.

Maybe a dozen times we drove forwards or backwards at express speed, by which time we could see that the herd was becoming restive and the master-bull distinctly annoyed. The bison were within thirty yards and less of us; they made attempt after attempt to cross the track. Then the bull uttered a shrill, whistling sound and pawed the ground, shaking his monstrous horns at our driver with increasing anger. Then we let him pass. The herd presented an imposing sight when it finally thundered across.

The morning mists had not yet lifted when, little further on, we came upon a sambar stag grazing in the open, and still further two barasingha stags wanted to do just the opposite—cross over the open country.

In both our cases our official followed the same tactics, driving the Land Rover backwards and forwards to prevent them. This allowed my companions to take some good photographs. Finally we drove on and allowed the stags to go where they wished.

The usual herds of spotted deer and blackbuck were everywhere, accompanied by families of peafowl, and we were all in high spirits that morning by the time we got back for breakfast. At lunch our friend had a pleasant surprise for us. He announced that a tiger had killed a buffalo-bait he had ordered to be tied up the previous day. So our official inquired if we would like to accompany him on elephantback to try to see the tiger, and of course we all agreed. Thereupon he ordered all three elephants to be got ready, one for ourselves, one for another party of visitors who had arrived that morning, and the third for a young German and his wife who had also just turned up.

We sent the elephants ahead and followed in half an hour in our Land Rover, with two jeeps from the Forestry department carrying the other people. We found the elephants awaiting us in a shady section of jungle and transhipped. Our official rode with us on the largest. Following each other in single file, the three elephants approached the buffalo kill.

As is the case very often, the carcass was not where it should have been, and where it had been lying a couple of hours earlier when the scout for the forestry department had spotted it and come to report its death. In all probability, the tiger had spotted the scout in turn, and no sooner had the man departed than the tiger had succeeded in breaking the buffalo's tethering rope and dragging the dead animal away. The ground was thickly covered with dried leaves, but from my perch upon the elephant I could detect no signs of a drag-mark. It looked as if the tiger had not dragged his victim away after all, but had shifted it bodily by carrying the kill across its back.

Some tigers adopt this strategy when they want to be particularly secretive, so leaving no drag-marks behind. Others prefer it as being more convenient than a kill that is dragged along the ground and gets caught by bushes and thorns. In the former case instinct appears to tell them that its is more difficult to trace a kill that has been carried away rather than one that has been dragged, while in the latter case it is entirely a matter of convenience.

As there were no thorns and scarcely any bushes at this spot, its was apparent the tiger had carried its kill away to prevent it from being traced by the scout whom he had seen snooping around. There was also another possible reason: the disquieting fact that there were hide-hunters in the Kanha Sanctuary (just as there were at Gir), who remove the hides of animals killed by carnivora in order to sell them. Perhaps this tiger had already lost some of his kills in this way and was taking no chances.

The practice of removing natural kills can have disastrous consequences. When the killer is frightened away, he does not return to his kill. Thus he is getting less food than normal and he is forced to kill some other jungle animal unnecessarily, or a domestic animal (as so frequently happens in Gir), which enrages the owner and leads to retaliation against the carnivore. Moreover, after the skin has been removed, it is a strong temptation to the skinner to poison the raw carcass lying exposed in the jungle. Deadly poison—in the form of Folidol—is very easy to obtain on the explanation that it is required as preventive against crop pests, for which purpose it is supplied plentifully by the government. Also, it is so very cheap. The owner of the cow reasons that his beast has cost time and a great deal of money, and that after consuming the poison the killer will not be able to wander far and will soon die. Then the grazer will take the tiger skin, too, and the money obtained for it will help to defray the loss sustained by the death of the milch cow.

Anyway, to carry its kill particularly a buffalo, this particular tiger must have been a large and powerful specimen. No cub, and very few tigresses, could accomplish such a task.

I dismounted from the elephant to examine the ground. A freshly broken leaf above waist-level and, a little further, a snapped green twig at about the same height, confirmed that the tiger had indeed carried the buffalo away bodily. There being a thick carpet of dried leaves on the grounds, no pugmarks were discernable; had the tiger dragged away its kill the dried leaves would have revealed it.

The tiger had headed directly downhill. The official whispered that a small stream, holding water in places, wound around the base of the hillock where we now stood. It was about a furlong away. With little doubt, the tiger had made for the stream.

I remounted the elephant, and spreading out to a distance of a hundred yards from one another, the three elephants with their parties now moved slowly downhill in line. The elephant on which my friend and I were riding was in the centre; the German and his wife were to our right, and the other party to our left. A belt of thick-growing green trees revealed the presence of the stream, and as we reached the high bank overlooking it we heard a low growl to our right and were just in time to see the hindquarters of a tiger in full flight with its tail. The German couple heard the growl too, and from their position to our right had a clear view of the tiger as it came bounding along the streambed. The next instant it saw them, changed direction abruptly, and scrambled up the further bank of the *nullah*, to vanish from sight.

Down below us lay the half-eaten remains of the dead buffalo within a foot of a pool of water trapped in the drying bed of the stream. Of the tiger we heard or saw no more. Much disappointed, we returned to where we had left the Land Rover and the two jeeps, changed into them, and were soon back at the guest house. In the afternoon we were on our way back to Nagpur.

On our journey we came to a large tank that was on the verge of drying up. Although there had been rain at Nagpur and Kanha, the area midway appeared to be suffering from drought. The entire village population had turned out and men, women and children of all ages were a foot deep in water, scooping the helpless fish into their baskets. Some of these were quite big, weighing four to five pounds each.

It was two in the morning when in drizzling rain we caught the plane from Nagpur to Calcutta. We were not scheduled to spend any time in Calcutta on this stage of our journey; we were to catch the next flight to Jorhat, a town in northeastern Assam, in an area known as the North-East Frontier Agency, from where we would have to drive by car to India's greatest game sanctuary, Kaziranga, to see the famous one-horned rhinoceros in its wild state, in addition to wild buffalo, barasingha, tiger and elephant.

I approached the booking-clerk to verify our seats on this plane and book our luggage, when he blandly told me that the official concerned would attend to this work only at 6.15 a.m. The flight to Jorhat was scheduled for 7.05 a.m.

The one thing passable about the Calcutta airport is its dining-room. We had tea there and waited till the clerk arrived. He scanned a list and said our names were not among those of the passengers on the Jorhat flight. He admitted we had been 'booked', but that was not enough; our names had not been 'confirmed'. Mere booking was not enough, he said. Any clerk could 'book' your name. But the airline authorities had to 'confirm' that there was a place for you on the plane. For us this had not been done. And the plane was already full.

He advised us to wait another fifteen minutes or so. The airline coach would be coming from the city, which was nine miles away, bringing the passengers for this flight. Our luck might be good. Maybe four persons had cancelled their flights, in which case there would be room for us.

The coach turned up at 6.30 a.m. What was more wonderful, four seats were available! Then an official asked to see our 'permits'.

'What permits?' we asked in unison.

'What permits?' he repeated. 'Don't you know that you are all foreigners? Foreigners are not allowed to enter the N.E.F.A. area without a permit signed by an official of the government of India as represented by the Assamese office in Calcutta, because Jorhat is close to the Nagaland border, where foreigners are not allowed.'

We did not know, and said so with some heat. We wanted to go to Kaziranga to look at rhinos, and were not bothered about N.E.F.A. or Nagaland. He shrugged and said we could not board the plane. Then he turned away.

Joe, one of our American friends, was a professional photographer. He had made the journey to India to take pictures and publish them in a series of articles about animals. Every moment was of consequence to him in terms of money. He really blew his top at the news. The airline official merely smiled. 'You will not be able to go to the Assamese office in the city today,' he added. 'You see, there is a general strike in progress and you will not be able to get a taxi. All motor traffic is off the road.'

'You might walk the nine miles,' he went on, 'but the office is certain to be closed, due to the strike.'

Yet, in spite of the gloomy picture he had painted we had a little luck. We succeeded in finding a conveyance to the city. It took us to one of the largest and best hotels in Calcutta, where we were fortunate to find accommodation. The strike that had been threatened did not materialize, but a *hartal* (which amounts to the same thing) was in progress. We managed to get a taxi and went posthaste to the office of the representative of the Assamese government for our permits. Here our passport numbers were noted and questions asked. We were told it would take a day or two for counterchecks to be made before the required permits could be given. Joe again blew his top. We just managed to get him out of the office in time. A few seconds more, and we would never have got those permits.

We decided to fill in the time while waiting by seeing as much as we could of Calcutta. Then it would not be necessary for us to stop over when returning from Jorhat.

We visited the zoo first. There we saw the three famous white tigers and their three half-grown white cubs. Light grey almost white in colour, they are certainly unique. One of the tigers is a beast of outsize proportions. Each of the six animals is housed in separated quarters. Then there is a *gayal*, a large animal with the body of a bison but with straight horns. It comes from eastern Assam and the Burmese border. Also, of course, the Indian rhino and a number of Gir and African lions. A feature of the zoo is a large lake within its boundaries to which great numbers of wild-duck of all varieties, migrants from beyond the Himalayas, find their way and spend four months of the year.

For the time being Joe was happy and seemed to have got over his irritation at the delay in reaching Kaziranga. But his pleasure was short-lived, for when we got back to the hotel at 5.30 p.m. we received the bad news that Indian Airlines had suspended all their flights to and from Calcutta owing to another *hartal*, called with immediate effect, due to the resignation of the West Bengal government.

The news made Joe furious. He wanted to charter a special plane to Kaziranga or go by car. Since neither of these things could be done, he became grumpy and sulky. The situation grew rather unpleasant.

All this happened on Monday, March 16, 1970. The last we heard before dinner was that, if the local government could sort itself out, we might be able to fly to Jorhat on the 7.05 a.m. flight on Wednesday, the 18th—if the permits came by then.

Tuesday (the 17th) was an uneventful day. We did some sightseeing by taxi in the morning and called at a few shops. By afternoon, however, the political situation had deteriorated; taxis were off the road and were replaced by truckloads of armed policemen patrolling the streets. We were warned not to attempt to step out of the hotel. Calcutta is crammed with over a million-and-a-half homeless people who dwell on the pavements. They cook and eat there, sleep there, and of course hardly ever get the opportunity to wash. It is unsafe for anybody to go out on the streets on foot during periods of political trouble of any sort, for these pavement-dwellers are not slow to take advantage of the first opportunity that comes their way, and when law and order go awry, to knife a passer-by in the back. They have no interest in the contesting political factions.

The only ray of hope that reached us that afternoon was in the form of our four permits. Frankly, I had not expected these to arrive for a long time. We ate our dinner early and retired, to wake up before 5 a.m. and get ready for the air journey we hoped to make at seven.

I had to carry my own suitcase and airbag down the stairway from the third floor, as the lift was not working. Nor were the servants willing to be helpful in this hotel, because of the rule that they must not be tipped. The airlines office was a bedlam. Nobody would pay us the least attention and it was impossible to find out whether we could proceed on the 7.05 a.m. plane, or even if that plane was taking off. The airport was another bedlam. Nobody knew if our names were on the list of passengers.

Seven o'clock, then eight and finally three in the afternoon. We were still firmly upon mother earth. None of us had lunch and we were all exhausted—what with Joe wanting to do this thing and that, claim a refund in court, send a telegram to the President of India with copies to the Prime Minister and the American Consulate, and the incessant chattering of the Bengalis around us, which reminded me of the noise made by the thousands of mynah-birds when they return in the evenings to roost on the tall trees surrounding my home at Bangalore. It was a nerve-wracking experience.

Nobody could say at what time our flight to Jorhat would take place ; indeed, nobody knew whether the plane would fly or not. To make matters worse, the officials suddenly received instructions from their union to go on a 'work to rule strike', while the porters were told to go on 'total strike'.

At last, at 3.15 p.m., the loudspeaker crackled, somebody coughed, and prepared to speak. Flight no. 211 was cancelled! We were lucky to find a taxi to take us back and drop us at the hotel from which we had started early that morning.

Being of a stubborn sort, I made a jaunt on my own to the airlines office the same evening, to find that our luck had changed at last. All four of us were booked on flight no. 249 at 6.10 the following morning, Thursday the 19th. Returning to the hotel in triumph, I found I had lost my old room; someone else had already taken it.

We left at 4.45 a.m. the following morning to find Dum Dum Airport in the same state of strike and confusion. The fate of flight no. 249 was greatly in the balance. However, with the use of much animal cunning, elbow grease and some surreptitious *baksheesh*, we managed to work a transfer to a combined flight of nos. 205 and 249 in a Viscount aircraft which, seemingly to the surprise of the airport officials themselves, and most assuredly to our own, took off at last at 9.30 a.m. None of us glanced earthwards at Calcutta as we left the city behind.

Five

The Anaibiddahalla Tigress

'ANAIBIDDAHALLA' LITERALLY MEANS IN THE VERNACULAR 'THE hollow into which the elephant fell.'

A stream winds downwards in southerly direction, having its source quite close to the forest hamlet of Kempekerai in the mountainous jungle stretch to the north of the town of Pennagaram in the district of Salem in Tamilnadu—formerly the Madras Presidency. This stream drops sharply at one point. It is a fall of about two hundred feet and it occurs in the region of granite rocks, so that the water has worn a deep hollow through striking the streambed over a period of perhaps thousands of years.

In the rainy season the water fills this hollow and rushes madly onwards in its course, but in summer, when the stream ceases to flow, a deep pool of still, dark and forbidding water fills the hole. Nobody knows its exact depth. Probably it is well over thirty feet. As summer advances and the heat increases, the level of the pool descends, leaving a sheer, circular wall of smooth rock all around, covered with slime and moss, up which nothing that has fallen into the pool can ever hope to climb back to safety.

That is what gave the place its name. For an elephant came along one hot season in search of water. The animal came to the pool and must have extended its trunk to suck up some of the water. Probably the water was just out of reach. The elephant extended too far, slipped on the slimy sides skidding down into the pool.

Elephants are excellent swimmers, but nothing and no one except a fish can continue swimming for ever. Some cartmen who were travelling along the nearby road to Muttur heard the elephant's screams and gurgles of fear and suffocation. They left their carts, seated themselves on the rocks, around the pool and gloated over the drowning beast's efforts to escape.

It is said that the elephant made prodigious but vain efforts to get a foothold on these slimy rocks. It slipped back each time.

The cartmen were so interested that they lit fires on the rocks and camped there the whole night. The elephant finally disappeared beneath the surface with a last shriek and gurgle in the early hours of the morning. It took over a fortnight before sufficient gas could collect in the stomach to float the carcass to the top. By this time the stench was awful, and it grew worse and worse as the thick hide and flesh fell apart in decomposition to expose huge chunks of rotting meat.

After that no creature came near that pool for a very long time. That is, not for at least thirty years, when a tiger that had been roaming the area and had started to prey upon men repeated the whole act by slipping into the pool itself. But that's another story.

Tigers rarely remained in this area for long, yet it was in fact the bend in a regular 'tiger beat' that resembled a rather wide letter U if laid upon its left side, that is with the opening facing left. The lower side represents the bed of the Chinar river, from the point where it empties itself into the larger Cauvery and for a little over seven miles up its course. At what point the stream from the north, along whose course lies the deep pool of Anaibiddahalla, empties itself into the Chinar.

Tigers were occasionally in the habit of swimming across the Cauvery and wending a leisurely way up the course of the Chinar, killing what spotted deer, sambar or pig they could find, and an occasional heifer or buffalo at the cattle *pattis* at Panapatti and Muttur along the way, to turn northwards up the course of the Anaibiddahalla stream, skirting the big pool and climbing the hill above it. They then continued another seven miles as the crow flies till they reached the bed of another stream, euphemistically known as the 'Talavadi river' although it is really little more than a deep and rocky *nullah*, flowing westwards for perhaps fifteen miles to empty itself into the Cauvery river at a point maybe seven miles above where the Chinar river itself joins the Cauvery. The Talavadi stream, of course, is represented by the upper side of the letter U lying on its left side.

As I have related, these wandering tigers from across the Cauvery would stroll eastwards up the Chinar river, then turn northwards up the Anaibiddahalla stream and finally return westwards down the Talavadi *nullah* to reach the Cauvery and swim across it once more to the Kollegal bank on the opposite side.

It was interesting to note that the tigers always followed this course and never came in the opposite direction—that is, from the Talavadi to the Anaibiddahalla stream down to the Chinar and back to the Cauvery. I wandered across this

area for many years and found it always so. I even questioned
the poojarees who have spent all their lives in these forests,
and they said the same thing. It is one of those jungle mysteries
that appears to defy explanation.

These feline hunters had always been harmless, confining
themselves to hit and run raids on the cattle *pattis* that lay along
the beat if they were not lucky enough to find wild game.

What came in time to be called the 'Anaibiddahalla Tiger'
was no exception. In fact it was no tiger, but a tigress. She
would follow this beat approximately every four months. At
times the interval would be longer. From what people living
in the mud-and-wattle huts along the Cauvery told me, she
would take a month to six weeks to complete the journey.
Then they would find her pug-marks coming down the rocky
Talavadi watercourse, taking advantage of the cooler sandy
stretches that skirted the edges of the stream where the rushes
grew, and the tall clumps of the 'orchid' or 'muthur' grass,
till once again she had reached the banks of the Cauvery.
Here, as her pugs indicated, she had spent no time hesitating.
They led to the water's edge where, whether the season was
dry and the water low, or the monsoons had broken and the
Cauvery in flood, they would disappear from sight. The
tigress must have been a strong swimmer.

Clearly, she had her home on the Kollegal bank of the
river, probably in some cave at some lonely spot on one of
the lofty mountains that rose abruptly in tiers from the river
bank. Very definitely her mate was there too, for suddenly
she failed to return to her old beat and a whole year passed.
Even more than a year, in fact.

Then the tigress returned. Once more her familiar tracks
were seen on the sands of the Chinar river as it wound past
the cattle *patti* of Panapatti and this time she was not alone.
Two sets of pugs accompanied her, one upon each side. They

were small pugs, about the size of the tracks that would have been made by large Alsatian dogs. The tigress had brought her two cubs along.

It was most unfortunate that she had done this, for it brought trouble to the cattle, the herdsmen that attended them and finally to the tigress herself and her cubs.

The cattle that had been killed hitherto by passing carnivore, both tigers and panthers, had been few, and the herdsmen who attended them had not taken the matter very seriously. They could always get away with an occasional lie by telling the owner that the animal had died of a sudden sickness, or slipped and fallen down a *khud* or steep *nullah* and broken its neck.

But this tigress, finding the cattle many in number and comparatively sleek in condition, decided to settle down in the area with her two cubs. It was so much easier to kill and to feed her cubs upon fat heifer or buffalo calf than have to wander for miles in search of food and then perhaps find none: she would have to go to sleep on an empty stomach and, worse still, so would her cubs. She knew from experience that when they were in that condition, as large as they had grown, they would still persist in trying to drink milk from her and that was a very painful experience. For the cubs had long and sharp claws that would tear into the fur and skin of her belly, and they had grown sharp and strong teeth that bit into her udders.

Kills began to take place in quick succession now, on almost every third day, for the cubs had keen appetites. No longer could the excuse of sickness or an accident be put forward to account for missing animals. They became far too many. So the poojarees and other low-caste villagers, who comprised the herdsmen that attended on the large assortment of cattle and buffalo kraaled at Panapatti, sent out a call for help to my *shikari* and camp-follower, Ranga by name who lives at the small town of Pennagaram, about eight miles away.

I have told you something about Ranga in other stories. He and a poojaree named Byra and I had wandered in these forests, mile upon mile, for many years, and there was hardly a corner of any of them that was unknown to one or all of us. Byra had been a poacher, and he remained one till he died. Ranga was a far more versatile fellow. Starting as a poacher, he had climbed the ladder of status to that of cartman, *shikari,* cultivator, and finally to that of a miniature landlord. He had attempted to kill his first wife and gone to jail for it, because he made the mistake of getting caught. Profiting from this experience, he had murdered his second wife after making sure he would not get caught by leaving a complicated lead to her uncle. Thereafter, realising it would be far too much of a risk to attempt a hat-trick by murdering his third, he had solved the problem by marrying a fourth, leaving the two women as a check upon one another while he got tied up with a fifth.

Leaving this place of many marriages for the moment and returning to the subject of the tigress, Ranga received the call for help and took it very seriously. He had an old muzzle-loader in those days. But it was a good weapon, inasmuch as it had laid low many a sambar hind that Ranga had ambushed over a water hole in summer, many a spotted deer, doe or fawn that had come to drink at the same water hole, and many a wild pig that had been so daring as to wander into the sugar-cane fields near Pennagaram on a moonlit night. Ranga was certain that he could account for the tigress with his trusty firearm without any trouble at all.

He sent word by the men who had come to summon him that the herdsmen should carefully conceal the remains of the next cow or buffalo killed by the tigress with branches of trees so that vultures would not find and finish it, and then to call him immediately. He would come at once, keep watch over the carcass and finish off the tigress as soon as she had returned for a second meal.

The plan worked well up to a point. The tigress killed a buffalo and with her two cubs ate nearly half of it. The herdsmen concealed the remains under branches cut from nearby trees and sent for Ranga. Ranga came without delay, bringing his trusty matchlock.

The only fly in the ointment was that there was no convenient branch close enough to the carcass for him to build a *machan* upon which to sit up for the tigress. There had been one and only one, and it had been just in the right place. But the foolish herdsmen of Panapatti had lopped it down just to get at its leaves and smaller branches to cover the cadaver! Could they not have brought the leaves from somewhere else? The whole jungle lay before them for this purpose. They had been far too lazy. Why walk so far when a convenient bough was to be found so close at hand?

So Ranga had to look for another site for his *machan*. He found it. There was another branch on another tree. But it was from eighty to hundred yards away. The range was rather too far for a muzzle-loader, particularly at night when everything appears so distorted. Some of these old blunderbusses are wonderfully effective at impossible ranges for a shotgun to be of any good. But on a dark night, when it would be difficult to bring off a good shot even with the aid of torchlight the odds were stacked against Ranga.

The tigress came along with her cubs. Ranga had heard them coming. Soon he knew the tigress had started her meal; he could hear the growls made by the mother and her offspring as they quarrelled over the meat.

That was when he pressed the button of the electric torch he had tied with string to the barrels of his muzzle-loader.

The cells were probably half-exhausted, for Ranga said he could hardly pick up the eyes that shone back a whitish red in his direction. Trusting to luck he pressed the trigger.

There was the usual roar of the explosion, the bright flash of the ignited black gunpowder, and the heavy pall of smoke that covered the whole branch upon which he was seated. Ranga knew he had not missed. He could hear the tigress roaring loudly and angrily.

To reload the muzzle-loader in the darkness, balanced precariously on a hastily constructed and unstable platform, was not easy, but he managed it at last. The roaring had ceased when he timidly depressed the switch of the flashlight a second time, but now he saw nothing beyond the dim, dark blur of the carcass lying upon the ground. Of tigress or cubs there was no sign.

When daylight came, my henchman and the herdsmen, who had heard the shot at night and came from their huts, saw that the tigress must have been hit. There were drops of blood upon the ground, and later, by dint of careful stalking, they found the trail with smears and spots of blood on the grass and upon the leaves. It led downhill and across the Chinar, which at this time of the year carried running water hardly a foot in depth.

On reaching the further bank, a heavy outcrop of orchid-grass showed where the tigress and her two cubs had passed. More smears of blood upon the green stems indicated that the tigress had been hit somewhere in the right flank. There was no evidence that her right shoulder or thigh had been damaged, as the pug-marks she had left in the soft sand showed no signs of a limp, nor did the wound appear to be a serious one, as the blood trail was comparatively light. After the clump of orchid-grass, the tigress and her family had crossed a low thorny hill, on the further side of which the trail had petered out. Either the wound had gradually ceased to bleed, or a layer of fat or hide had worked itself across the cavity to stop the bleeding.

In the usual optimistic fashion of the Indians, Ranga and his companions congratulated each other that between them they had got rid of this troublesome animal. No doubt it would die of its wounds somewhere in the jungle or be drowned when it tried to swim back across the Cauvery in its weakened state. Of the fate of its two cubs they never thought or cared.

It was a dark night, just over two months later, when a string of bullock carts bumped and jangled down the three sharp hairpin bends in the track that led from the higher-levels of the hill above the Anaibiddahalla pool to the lush valley through which the little stream purled on its way to the Chinar. The vegetation was dense in this valley, and elephants and sloth bear, sambar and jungle-sheep abounded. The felines and spotted deer kept for the most part to the more open forest slightly higher up; the deer because they disliked getting into heavy vegetation where they could be easily ambushed by carnivore and the even more dangerous wild dogs, and the felines because the valley was full of insect pests and they hated the big ticks, the mosquitoes and, strangely enough, the tiny fleas that were a feature of this forest.

The leading bullock-cart carried a dimly burning lantern hanging from the yoke securing the two buffaloes that drew it ; it hung just behind their hindquarters. There was a reason for this. The domestic buffalo is an abnormally stupid animal. If the lantern had been suspended anywhere near its neck or face, it would refuse to draw the cart. Nobody knew just why. Maybe the beasts that drew the cart thought that they were home, so why go further? With the light behind them and darkness ahead, they thought they had still to go on. Rather

171

illogical reasoning, I admit, but maybe buffaloes are illogical creatures. The cartmen had to use them in preference to the usual bulls, for the loads of cut bamboos were unusually heavy and the track stoney and steep. Buffaloes have more strength than bulls.

Admittedly, to hang the light behind rather than in front had the obvious disadvantage. Nobody, not even the buffaloes, could see what lay ahead. And when there was only one lantern to the whole convoy of a dozen carts, it did not help. But perhaps it was better not to see too much, on the principle that to see no evil was to know no evil. What I mean is, an elephant might be standing just around the corner or just off the track. Ordinarily, he would not be visible at night. Also, ordinarily, unless he was a 'bad' elephant, he would take no notice of a string of bullock-carts passing by. So why see him unnecessarily and become unnerved?

However, this did not always work. If perchance the elephant was not so good, or even slightly bad, he might not relish this disturbance of his privacy. Yet there was nothing the cartmen could do about it anyway. They certainly could not turn back. Try turning a bullock cart around hurriedly on a narrow track on a pitch-black night, with eleven more carts and eleven friends driving them behind you. Of course they could all come to a halt instead; at least the leader could. Number two would bump into him and stop. Number three would bump into the number two and so on. Would it help? Better to keep going. If the beastly elephant comes too close, beat the empty kerosene tin in the cart behind you, kept there for just that purpose. That should stop him. And if it does not? Jump out of the cart and leg it down the line of carts behind you. But do not lose your head and run into the jungle; there may be another elephant there. By the time the elephant smashes up your cart, throws one or both your buffaloes into

172

the air in his exhilaration and then turns his attention to cart number two, you have enough time to be well out of the way. Besides, there are eleven other fellows behind you. By the time they wake up and realise all is not well, the elephant will have had a roaring time. The main thing is to save your own skin.

But what about snake? Poisonous snakes crossing the road? One of the buffaloes might step upon one; in which case, within two hours there would be only one buffalo less.

The cartman should always ride in his cart, not walk behind it for fear of elephants. One such cartman never kept to this rule. He had met a herd of elephants on this very track, but about seven miles further on. It had been evening and he had been alone in his cart; so he had returned to the camp of the bamboo-cutters, to set forth before dawn the next morning. This time he walked behind the cart, so that if he bumped into the elephant he could fade away without being spotted.

However, the buffaloes escaped treading on a cobra in the track, but one of the cartwheels broke its back. The next thing the cobra saw was the man's foot. So he bit it. The cartman walked another mile or so, reaching the Muttur forest bungalow, where I was encamped, at break of day. I cut the wound to bleed it, and walked him about vigorously.

All to no avail. The poor fellow died in about two hours, and the police gave me no end of trouble for two days. Apparently, the fact that I had cut his foot with a knife to cause bleeding was highly suspicious. Perhaps if I had done it with some blunt instrument and concealed the blood things would have been okay. I just could not get them to understand the reason. I think I have told this story somewhere else, but it suffers repetition as it has direct bearing on bullock-carts that travel through jungles by night.

However, no elephant ambushed this particular convoy. But a very hungry tigress did, accompanied by two equally hungry cubs. They let the convoy pass, that is all but one. They attacked the last cart.

The driver was sound asleep when it happened, hunched up over the scraps of rope he used as reins, and rolled up in a coarse black blanket. He awoke with a start, to the sensation of falling through space, as the cart toppled down into a *nullah* bordering the road. He could hear deafening sounds; growls, snarls and the bellowing of his own two buffaloes. He did not know it just then but riding on the back of one of them, with her fangs embedded in its throat, was a tigress. A cub, slightly less than half-grown, but ineffectually into its side, while another clung to the hindquarter of the other buffalo.

The cart and all the creatures involved in this melee landed with a crash at the bottom of the *nullah*, which was luckily not deep. The cartman was thrown free, while the yoke holding the buffaloes snapped. The buffalo that had been attacked by one of the cubs broke away and bolted down the *nullah*, leaving the bewildered cub to join its mother and the other cub that were attacking the remaining buffalo. In another two minutes it was dead.

The cartman, hastily extricating himself from the entangling blanket, saw struggling black forms and heard frightful noises. By the light of the stars he scrambled up the side of the *nullah* to regain the track the convoy had been following. Away in the distance he heard the jangling and thumping of the other carts as they raced away from the scene. Those of the drivers who had been awake and heard the pandemonium that had broken out behind them had guessed that something terrible was happening to their companion behind. Exactly to which companion they did not care nor stop to find out; the buffaloes yoked to the carts needed no goading to speed their pace. They knew the roars of a tiger when they heard them! Galloping behind each other in a jagged line, the convoy bounced and thudded down the precarious track, while running for his life, the luckless driver whose cart had been attacked ran behind to catch them up.

News of this event spread far and wide and the bullock-carts ceased to travel by night. This did not help the tigress, who became more hungry, and she had to feed her cubs besides herself. Nobody knew it then, but her right shoulder had been badly hurt; in fact, the bone was split by the lead ball from an old, old musket. It was Ranga's musket that had done the damage.

Driven by hunger, the tigress started to attack cattle by daylight. In this she was joined by her cubs, who were rapidly learning the art of killing, though the methods were crude and amateurish as befitted their inexperience. Their mother could not do much better, handicapped as she was by a smashed shoulder. Thus it transpired that each kill made by this trio of animals presented a nasty spectacle of mangled living flesh and torn hide and bone, a victim that had been partly eaten alive. It was all so different from the kill made by a normal tiger; a neat job in which the neck of the prey is neatly broken with a minimum of bloodshed.

These attacks continued for the best part of six months, during which time the cubs grew apace. They now required no help, but could kill expertly by themselves. Curiously, they remained with their maimed mother instead of breaking away and fending for themselves as cubs begin to do when about a year old. The killings of cattle and buffaloes increased as the cubs grew older and larger and their appetites increased.

Probably nothing more exciting would have happened had not Mariappa, the cowherd, instead of running away as fast as he could, as did all wise cowherds, rushed to defend his milch-cow when the three tigers attacked it at the edge of his field. He might have succeeded had the attacker been a single beast, but numbers bring courage, both to human being and to tigers.

If you should be 'ghooming' in a jungle—that is wandering about with the hope of seeing what animals you come across—or should you meet a pair of tigers or a tigress with cubs (both of which are today most unlikely to happen, I might tell you), halt and above all do not move. Do not start to run away, for that will attract the attention of the tigers which, just like your dog, love to chase things that run away from them. Take cover, by all means, if you know how, without floundering about and advertising your presence. Above all, remain absolutely motionless. And never, I strongly advise you, start to follow them to see where they are going. There is a fair chance that you can do this in perfect safety with a single tiger, or even with a pair of panthers. But when a pair of tigers are involved, or a mother with cubs, the chances are small. Tigers do not like their family privacy disturbed for one thing, while numbers definitely bolster their courage. With elephants it is quite the opposite. Leave 'Jumbo' alone if he is by himself, and avoid a female with a calf, though you can drive a herd of thirty like cattle almost with impunity, even if you are all by yourself.

Mariappa committed the grave error of rushing towards three tigers lying over the lovely cow which they had just killed. I suppose he thought he would be able to save it. Very brave of him, but equally foolish. The next instant he was dead. Which of the three felines killed him nobody knows.

Six

In a Jungle Long Ago

IT ALL HAPPENED AT PANAPATTI MANY YEARS AGO. *PATTI*, AS I HAVE
explained in earlier stories, signifies 'a cattle-camp', and
Panapatti was one such camp. It is situated on the southern
bank of the Chinar river, about three miles and a half from
its confluence with the Cauvery, which is the largest river in
southern India. The Chinar holds water only in the monsoons,
and possibly a couple of months after that. For the remaining
six months of the year it is a dry *nullah*, although both banks
for a dozen mile or more from where it empties itself into
the great river are clothed with heavy jungle, acres of bamboo,
with *muthee*, tamarind and *jumlum* trees and other varieties
in between.

When the monsoons end vegetation dries quickly in India.
As a consequence the grass and the stalks of *chollam, ragi* and
rice, harvested from the fields and given to the cattle after
the ears of grain have been removed, becomes exhausted too

and there is nothing for the domestic herds to eat. That is when the owners of the herds turn covetous eyes upon the forests, where the grass still grows and certain varieties of leaves and shrubs provide grazing.

Grazing licences are purchased from the forest department, and thousands of domestic cattle are driven into the jungle, where they are kept till the advent of the next monsoons, when they are driven back to the village again once local grazing becomes possible as the grass and crops spring up. As this is an annual performance regular campsites have grown up in all the forests where the cattle are kraaled during the summer months. These sites in the south are the 'pattis'.

Panapatti is in the district of Salem of what is now Tamil Nadu state and was formerly the Presidency of Madras; hardly anybody outside a radius of twenty miles knew or heard of its existence. To my knowledge on only two occasions did excitement in any form come to Panapatti. The first of these was with the advent of an elephant that killed a few people, including a hunter that had come after it. This animal came to be known as 'The Rogue Elephant of Panapatti'. I have told the story in an earlier book.*

There was a lull of several years after that. Then notoriety visited the little camp for the second time with the advent of 'The Avenging Spirit', which I am going to tell you about. Let me hasten to add that this spirit was not a human phantom but a tiger that appeared suddenly from nowhere, earned a ghostly fame, and then disappeared as mysteriously as it had come.

The owners of most of the herds kraaled at Panapatti were rich landlords inhabiting the large town of Dharmapuri, about twenty-eight miles away as the crow flies. Three or four, of

---

* See: *Nine Man-eaters and One Rogue.*

lesser importance, hailed from the smaller town of Pennagaram situated just ten miles distant. The herdsmen to whom the cattle were entrusted during their stay at *patti*, were the lowest caste of villagers from Pennagaram, augmented by a few 'poojarees', who were jungle-men belonging to an aboriginal tribe, living in the forest all the year round, sheltered in little thatched huts or in *gavvies* or hollows dug into the banks of the Chinar river at spots where that stream ran through hilly country and the banks were steep and high. This protected the inmates from elephants that crossed the Cauvery and walked up the bed of the Chinar river in the dark hours of the night.

Such a poojaree was Kaiyara. He had been one of the graziers regularly employed for quite a number of years in looking after the herds that came to Panapatti during the summer months. On an average the cattle remained in this camp for about six months in the year, and Kaiyara's wage was ten rupees (about 50p) for the entire period, plus a weekly allowance of rice or *chollam* or *ragi*. Not all together, mind you, for that would be gross over-payment. Say about ten pounds in weight per week, whichever grain was the cheapest available in the market at that time.

When Kaiyara had first taken service several years ago, he had had his wife with him and an only child, a daughter named Mardee. Then the krait came. It had been a very hot night and the slim, jet-black snake with the infrequent white notches across its neck and back, had slithered into the grass-thatched hut occupied by the little family and coiled itself around the base of the dark earthen pot in which the drinking water was kept. No doubt the reptile was feeling the heat, too, and relished the cool of the pot.

Kaiyara's wife had very long hair. When she lay on the floor of the hut at night, it had a habit of getting knotted or falling across her face and disturbing her. So on that occasion she had decided to tie it up with the strip of black rag that she kept for the purpose.

But where was that rag? By the water-pot. Talking to her husband as she did so, the woman stooped and her fingers closed around what she thought was the rag. Unfortunately it was the krait she had grasped.

The snake struck at what it thought was an enemy, burying its small fangs just above her wrist. Then it disengaged itself, slithered behind the water-pot and passed through the wattle hut wall into the jungle outside.

The woman hardly saw what had bitten her. Something cold and black, she knew, and then it was gone. She called to her husband and held out her arm for his inspection. Kaiyara looked and saw two tiny drops of red blood on her back skin. They were hardly half-an-inch apart. The poojaree recognized the marks for what they were, punctures inflicted by the fangs of a venomous snake.

He got busy. There was no doctor, no anti-venom injection, no hospital within twenty-eight miles. Only his dirty cloth bag, containing some powdered herbs and roots, could help.

Kaiyara knew nothing about lancing the wound and bleeding it. So he stepped outside, picked up some soft cow-dung, made a mixture of it with some of the powder from his bag, and smeared the paste thickly over the wound. Then he started muttering a mantra, over and over again.

Within thirty minutes his wife complained of great pain in her wrist. Also shooting pains in her abdomen. She said she was beginning to feel giddy. After another thirty minutes she could not speak. The last she had said was that she had great pains in her stomach. Saliva was pouring from the corners of her mouth. Her breathing was heavy. Yet another

180

thirty minutes later there was hardly any sign of breathing. The woman was cold and limp. Her eyes had rolled back in their sockets. A few minutes more and she was dead. Kaiyara was left alone with his little girl, Mardee, to look after.

The years passed. Mardee was now a comely lass. She had grown into full womanhood, mature and well developed in body. Handsome, too for a poojaree aboriginal. She was her father's mainstay and looked after him well, cooking all the meals and doing the chores in their tiny household. She also went out with the cattle at dawn and grazed them till sunset, returning with the herds of beasts as they ambled home in the evenings when the sun sank behind the jagged hillocks to the west on the bank of the Chinar.

Many of the poor herdsmen and a number of the poojarees coveted her and came to Kaiyara with proposals of marriage. To strengthen their suits, some were prepared to forego the usual dowry which every father had to pay the bridegroom and his family before a daughter could be married. Mardee spurned all her suitors. Young as she was, the girl was of a determined nature; she would have nothing to do with common herdsmen or poojarees.

Then one day, Sathynarayan came to Panapatti. He was the eldest son of his father, Gopalswamy of Dharmapuri, a rich landlord and merchant who owned over two hundred head of cattle grazing at Panapatti. Sathynarayan was also married and had a wife and young son. But they stayed behind at Dharmapuri when he came to Panapatti to inspect his father's herd. Sathynarayan arrived at a comfortable time of the morning when the herds had already been taken out for graze: about nine o' clock. The cattle had been driven out as the sun's rays were just rising above the Muttur Ridge, four miles to the east, to melt away the heavy mists that clothed the valley of the Chinar and the sloping land on both its banks, and to send the wild elephants into the dense bamboos for shelter, and the sambar into the hills.

He left his car on the main road with his chauffeur and walked the two miles of jungle track that brought him to the *patti*. It was a filthy track, Sathynarayan thought; the earth was several inches deep in layers of cow-dung, deposited year after year by successive herds of cattle and buffaloes. He stepped delicately, avoiding the more recent patches of dung for fear of soiling his shoes.

Soon he stood at the doorway of Kaiyara's hut and coughed loudly; then he spat. It was utterly beneath his dignity to call the inmate by name. The poojaree had watched his employer's son approaching. He crawled through the low doorway and prostrated himself on hands and knees, touching his forehead to the ground, the customary salutation of a poojaree in the old days.

'What news?' inquired the young man curtly.

'All is well, *Swamy*,' replied the poojaree regaining his feet. 'By the grace of the gods, none of your revered father's cattle have been taken away by the ferocious wild beasts that fill this forest nor stricken by the cursed foot-and-mouth sickness. I give thanks daily to the gods for their mercy. The animals have been driven out to graze under the care of my unworthy daughter.'

'So that is how you earn your keep?' asked Sathynarayan pointedly. 'By sending the cattle out in charge of a girl while you sleep in your hut. What can she do if a wild animal should attack?'

The father was silent, then he thought of a brilliant excuse: 'I was sick of the fever, with pains in my stomach and diarrhoea all last night, your honour, else I would have gone with the herd myself.

182

'You lie!' accused the landlord's son. 'However, as I have come to see the animals for myself, you must now guide me to where your daughter has driven them.'

Thus it came about that Sathynarayan saw Mardee for the first time and lusted after her greatly. He could not speak to her straightaway. That would have been beneath his status, particularly with her father looking on. He would have to look for some better opportunity.

The young man took a great interest in his father's herd after that day. His parent was rather surprised suddenly to discover that his son-and-heir, who had hitherto shown little liking for his business and none whatever for cattle, had developed an unexpected thirst for knowledge. So he smiled indulgently and decided to encourage his son. Probably it was just a passing fad and would soon wear off, when the boy would become as useless as before. Of course Sathynarayan's wife could not comment. Women in India are not permitted to question the comings and going of their men.

Sathynarayan timed his visits to a later hour, when he knew the animals would be grazing in the forest. Moreover, he avoided the *patti* and went directly to the grazing ground. Thus he met Mardee for the second time, and third and fourth time, and many times thereafter.

Although she was still a child, her woman's instinct told the poojaree girl that the young man had fallen in love with her, a sentiment which he was not slow to encourage with small gifts of money. Mardee had always aimed high, far above the local cattleboys and poojarees, and here was the answer to her dreams. A very rich young man; her employer's only son to boot!

Sathynarayan lost no time in seducing her. The jungle offered plenty of scope for that and Mardee became pregnant. Of course, the lovers thought that nobody knew of their clandestine affair. Actually everybody in the *patti* knew about it. The herd-boys had seen from a distance. The poojarees had gone one better: they had stalked the lovers and peeped on their most intimate moments at close range. Then they had run back and told Kaiyara.

The old man was astounded. Such a thing was unheard of; it had never happened before. His employer's son was a brahmin of the highest caste. Moreover, he had his own wife and son. Mardee, his own daughter, as a poojaree was of the lowest caste! How could this thing be? If he should dare to question the young man, the matter would be reported, and his employer, the father, would undoubtedly throw Kaiyara out of his job. So he kept the matter to himself for five months until it was evident his daughter was going to have a baby. He questioned the girl. To his dismay, she appeared to be not in the least ashamed. She admitted that Sathynarayan was the father and declared he was in love with her and had promised to marry her.

At the very next opportunity Kaiyara screwed up enough courage to question the young man.

Sathynarayan flew into a towering rage. 'What are you talking about?' he thundered. 'Would I defile myself with your daughter, a slut of the lowest caste, like yourself? Who told you this absurd tale?'

'She told me herself' answered the old man flatly.

Sathynarayan scowled, but said nothing in reply. He turned his back and walked away.

The next morning Mardee took the herd out again for grazing. It was clear she had not slept the night before. There were rings under her eyes and they were red. She had been crying. This could be understood, for her father had said that the young man had denied having touched her and had called her a low-class slut.

It was long past the sunset hour when the herd struggled back that evening. They came in twos and three, and a few of them did not come at all. And of Mardee there was no trace.

Darkness fell before Kaiyara fully realized what had happened. He begged the other men to come with him in search of his daughter. Some agreed. Others pleaded that they were indisposed.

There were no lanterns in the *patti*. Nor did anyone possess an electric torch. Each little hut had just one small oil-light of its own, a tiny taper of wick, floating in a little earthenware bowl of oil. There was no moonlight either, for it was time of *amavasa*, the darkest period of the month. Moreover, this is also the most inauspicious and dangerous period to be out at night, the time when devils of all kinds roam at will: evil spirits that sometimes appear as men and women, sometimes as elephants, tigers and other wild animals, and often as tall white pillars reaching to heaven. They would cackle and scream with unholy laughter when they came across defenceless mortals to kill.

In this atmosphere of terror the little party set forth, treading their way along the trails left by the cattle as they grazed in the forest. The only lights came from the stars that blinked down through the foliage. Inky darkness covered the ground. A demon might be anywhere, behind tree-trunk or bush, and might strike at any moment. A tiger or panther might lurk round any corner. Even an elephant could be three paces away and would be entirely hidden in that gloom. The men walked together, in a bunch, those at the sides making considerable noise as they brushed through the thorns bordering the pathways and getting their skins well lacerated in the process because nobody wanted to be the last man in line.

It was common knowledge that it was the last man who always fell prey to the attack of a tiger, a panther or an elephant.

At least, if that happened, he would cry out and warn the others, who would have a chance to run away. But if a demon attacked him he would just disappear in silence. Nobody would know about it. Then the next last man would vanish, and the next, and so on. No one would know a thing till all had disappeared.

In this fashion the little party crept forward, faltered and then came to a stop. Each member had worked himself into a state of abject fear and the feeling was infectious. By mutual consent they came to a halt.

'Mardee', screamed her father in desperation. 'Mardee, Mardee, where are you my child?'

There was no answer but the sough of the jungle breeze as it began to blow down the valley. Far away a tiger roared. Just ahead an elephant heard the roar and trumpeted in challenge. A sambar stag on the further bank of the Chinar caught the scent of human beings and belled in alarm. Once, twice and many times. A langur monkey, higher up the hillside, woke to the disturbing noises and grated his repeated warning to the other members of his tribe.

The search party wavered no longer. They turned and hastened back to the *patti*. Indeed, they walked so fast it was impossible to do so in a bunch. Somebody had to be last. But this time the gods were good: no wild beasts attacked him, nor did a demon strike him down. They all got back to the *patti*, but without Mardee.

As the girl had vanished in broad daylight, everybody thought she had been taken by a tiger. Had an elephant killed her, or a panther for that matter, some trace of her would have been found. But although Kaiyara, and every other resident of the *patti*, combed the surrounding jungle for a week, not a trace of the missing girl did they come across.

Then there came a clue. A lone cartman, struggling to get his vehicle up the steep incline of the Muttur track leading through the jungle to Pennagaram, remembered that he had been forced off the roadway into the ditch by a big car that had come up from behind and was trying to get ahead of him. Because of the gradient, all carts were hauled by buffaloes, as they were more sturdy than the customary bullocks, and more sure-footed. Unfortunately, they were also more stupid. When the car had come up from behind, the cartman had noticed that, strangely, the driver had not even once sounded his horn. Instead, he had attempted to overtake the cart in swift silence, with the result that the buffaloes had shied and run down into the steep ditch beside the road, capsizing the vehicle with its load of bamboos. Luckily, the cartman had been thrown clear, and as he hit the ground he had looked up to see who was responsible for this callous behaviour.

The car was Sathynarayan's. The cartman knew it well by sight. Somebody else was driving but he recognized Sathynarayan in the back seat. He had been holding on to a woman. He had caught a glimpse of a red sari as the car lurched past at high speed. He said he did not know who the woman was. But Mardee had been wearing a red sari on the day she disappeared. Slowly the pieces of the puzzle came to fit together.

Normally, one could expect the Muttur track to be deserted in the early hours of the morning. The presence of the carman was something unexpected. If a car were parked at a bend in the track where it wound around a stony hillock called Karadimedu (Bear's Mill), the owner could follow a short cut through the forest that would take him in about twenty minutes to the grazing ground where Mardee had driven the cattle.

The whole thing seemed to lead to a choice of two conclusions. Either the lovers had made an appointment which the rich young man had used as an opportunity to abduct her, perhaps with the intention of murdering her later; or unknown to her, he came upon her by stealth and had taken her away against her wish.

Kaiyara reasoned all this out in his mind aided by one or two of his companions whom he felt he could trust. He dared not speak of it openly. There were informers everywhere and none knew who could be trusted. Word would be carried to the young man, or his father, Gopalswamy. Kaiyara would then be sacked. That would be the least that could happen. He remembered he was up against moneyed people. They could pay *goondas* (ruffians) to beat him up, perhaps murder him. For that matter, they could bring a false charge against him of theft or something else. He would be locked up in the police station and be beaten up mercilessly. His cronies advised him to leave well alone. Treat the whole matter as the will of God, and forget about it.

But Kaiyara was a father. Further, he held a reputation at least among the herdsmen and his brother poojarees at Panapatti, of being a black magician who could cast powerful spells, and if he did nothing he would lose the reputation for good and all. He would be scorned as an imposter, a coward. His companions would say to each other: he called himself a black magician, but where is his magic now? If he were genuinely what he claimed to be, he would cast a spell upon the man who had committed this crime and that man would fall very sick and die. For everybody at the *patti* had reasoned out for himself what had happened, although none dared to speak of the matter openly.

A few days later, the night of *amavasa* came again, the darkest night of the month, when evil spirits are afoot and magicians cast their most potent spells. When the camp fire burned fitfully at Panapatti after the evening meal and the herdsmen sat around to chat for a few minutes before retiring to their huts for the night, Kaiyara stepped into their midst and addressed them. He had adorned himself for the occasion. Red and white marks changed his face into a fearsome sight. A silver armlet above his right elbow identified his status as a black magician. A necklace of the large serrated seeds of the *oudarrachamani* plant encircled his neck, and another of large, black, glass beads.

He cleared his throat and began to speak: 'Brothers, as you all know some evil man has beguiled my daughter. Not only has he done wrong, but he has taken her away and perhaps murdered her. The days are bad and we are poor people. There is none we can approach for help. None will stretch forth a finger to aid us, for we have no money, while the evil man who has done this thing is very, very rich. But I do have this power which neither he nor all his money, influence and friends can take away from me. It is the power to curse him and his family, from the realms of the living to those of the dead. I will go in search of my beloved daughter. Maybe I will find her, maybe not. Maybe, I myself will not return. Should any harm befall me at the hands of this evil man, I want you to bear witness that I now curse him and his family. His life, and the lives of his dear ones, will be swallowed up for the life of my beloved daughter and my own. I curse him! I curse him! I curse him! By this thrice repeated curse, it shall be as I say.'

Next morning Kaiyara went forth from the *patti*. Only his close companions knew he had gone to Dharamapuri boldly to announce to his employer, the rich businessman and cattle-owner, what Sathynarayan had done to his daughter.

Kaiyara never came back. He was never seen again! The herdsmen soon forgot about him and the words he had uttered. Possibly his special friends thought about it and felt sorry. The poojaree had been foolish enough to put his head into the tiger's mouth, so to say.

Six months passed. It was the festival of Pongal and everybody was enjoying themselves. In the village the bullocks' horns were gaudily painted, red, blue, green, bright yellow. Upon their foreheads were long red and white marks of ochre too. Games were arranged and sometimes mock fights between men and bulls.

Sathynarayan and his wife and son, accompanied by his father, motored from Dharamapuri through Pennagaram to the point on the road where they had to leave the car in the care of the driver and walk the distance to Panapatti.

In fact this trip had been entirely the father's idea. Sathyanarayan certainly did not want to go to Panapatti ever again. The place held too many awkward memories for him. That damned poojaree girl had taken him seriously. She had actually believed the silly stories he had spun that he was going to marry her and make a lady out of her. To make matters worse, the wretched girl had the misfortune to become pregnant, and to crown matters she had told her father all about it. The affair had cost him a thousand rupees, which he had to pay to the chauffeur, Das, to gain his silence about the day they had abducted the bitch. Luckily not even Das knew what he had done with her body. He had made the driver get out of the car so that there would be no witness.

As if that were not bad enough, the damned girl's father had had the temerity to come all the way to their family home at Dharamapuri to inquire about his daughter's whereabouts. By a stroke of good fortune, his father had gone to Madras the day before. That incident had cost him another thousand rupees. This time Das knew, for it had been Das who had taken the dead body late at night in the spare car. He and the driver had weighted it with stones and the latter had dragged it out of the car and thrown it into a large tank forty miles away, along the road to Salem.

But all this meant that Das knew too much. Last week the driver had approached him with a demand for five hundred rupees. Sathynarayan had started to refuse, but had stopped short when he saw the smirk upon the driver's face which told its own tale.

Then Sathynarayan made a plan. Immediately after Pongal he would go for a big shoot, and he would take Das with him. There would be a shooting accident and the driver would be killed! Of course, a lot of awkward questions would be asked by the police, but he knew that his father would come forth with bags of money and the questioners would fall silent.

Now why, of all place, did his father want to visit Panapatti for the Pongal festival? Sathynarayan had tried to put the old man off. But as everybody knows, old people are very stubborn. His parent had got quite hot about it. He had even chided the young man with the disappointment he had felt when the latter's sudden interest in the cattle herd at Panapatti had as suddenly ended. And so the four of them were trudging through the jungle to Panapatti, having left Das to look after the car. The chauffeur had worn another of his nasty smirks as he caught his eye before parting. Sathynarayan resolved that he would have to stage that hunting trip and the accident that was to go with it, without further delay. Das was becoming far too dangerous.

The four visitors reached the *patti* where the herdsmen and the few poojarees had made ready to welcome them. As the august patrons were of the highest caste no refreshments of any sort could be prepared by them or pass through their defiled hands before being presented. Thus the gifts took the form of green coconuts, which had to be broken before the water could be drunk, and huge sweet-limes called 'sathgoodies', from which the outer skin had to be removed to get at the pulp. Gifts of this sort would be readily accepted, as there was no chance of the ingredients being contaminated.

The painted and gaudily decorated cattle were displayed and a couple of mock-fights between men and bulls were staged. As the animals were roped and held in restraint by half-a-dozen men on each side, these encounters were farcical and excited nobody except perhaps those who took part in them. The evening closed with the usual felicitations and, after consuming more coconut water, the visitors prepared to depart. They had taken care to ascertain from the herdsmen that there were no elephants in the vicinity and so they dawdled till a later hour than they would otherwise have done. Once again the sun was sinking behind the jagged hills across the western bank of the Chinar, but with normal walking they would reach the main road where the car awaited them before dusk.

It happened somewhere midway between the *patti* and the main road. Sathynarayan and his father were walking ahead together, probably discussing a business deal of some sort. The young man's wife, as behoves all respectable and dutiful Indian married women, was obliged to walk a few paces to the rear. This she was doing, leading her small boy by the hand. The child was tired and bored to death by the whole proceeding. He was crying.

It is not good for the young of any creature to cry in the forest. The jungle recognizes no law of pity for the young and helpless, only the rule of the survival of the fittest, which certainly does not include the young. There was a sudden snarl; at the same time a great tawny body with black stripes materialized from nowhere to seize the crying child in its jaws. The mother saw this and instinctively hurled herself at the beast's head to save her child. The two men in front heard the snarl and swung around. They saw the tiger with the child in its mouth rear up and strike the mother with its front paws. They waited to see no more.

Sathynarayan, who was younger, ran faster and reached the car first. His father fell from exhaustion several times before he also made it. Then Das drove the car at breakneck speed to Pennagaram to get help. No help was forthcoming at that hour, for the shades of night had already fallen. The next morning a vast concourse of people armed to the teeth, retracted the steps of the fleeing men and came upon the tragedy.

Mother and the son lay a yard apart. The tiger's great teeth had bitten through and through the little boy. His mother had been killed by the two great blows that had been dealt to her. Not a morsel of flesh had been eaten from either victim. Upon the hard ground were no traces of pug-marks.

As may be imagined, pandemonium reigned at Pennagaram and in the nearby villages and forest *pattis*. No man-eating tiger or panther had been heard of for a hundred miles around. As a matter of fact, at this particular time the herdsmen of Panapatti and the fishermen at Uttaimalai and Hogenaikal and the other hamlets on the other banks of the great Cauvery river confirmed that there was a distinct lack of carnivores of any sort in the area. Being the dry season, and this year a particularly hot one, the sambar had taken themselves to the mountains and the spotted deer had gone to less dry area. Such carnivore as had existed, and these were few, had gone with them.

Where the killer had come from, nobody could tell. Why he had killed and then not eaten was a still greater mystery.

I had been on a visit to my land at Anchetty, a hamlet in the same forest but about twenty miles to the north when all this happened, but no news had reached Anchetty yet. I had later left Anchetty, walked to another *patti* named

Gundalam, and then sixteen miles down the course of a stream I have called the 'Secret river' to its confluence with Cauvery river. From there I had come another ten miles to Uttaimalai, where the fishermen were very excited at having heard of the happenings near Panapatti.

There is a short cut across the foothills which brought me to the bed of the Chinar river two furlongs below Panapatti. I found the herdsmen and poojarees gathered under a tree discussing the recent event. They had not driven the herds of cattle into the forest for grazing for the last two mornings for fear the killer might attack either the animals or themselves—that is, the one or two herdsmen who felt that such a thing might happen, and they were in the minority.

All the poojarees, without exception, and the rest of the herdsmen were of the opinion that they and the herds were quite safe. The tiger that had killed was not a man-eater, for it had not touched the bodies of the woman and child it had slain! Nor was it a game-killer, for they had come across no bones or carcases of sambar or spotted deer. The vultures had not soared in the sky nor quarrelled over the remains of a kill for a long time.

In fact, this was not a tiger or a panther at all—at least, not one of flesh and blood! It was the spirit of Kaiyara, the poojaree, who had avenged the murder of his only daughter and of himself. The poojaree had assumed the form of a tiger to fulfil the curses he had placed upon the braggart Sathynarayan.

'Nor is this the end, *dorai*,' the eldest of the poojarees at the *patti*, and one who had been a particular crony of Kaiyara's, confided to me in an undertone. 'Not by a long chalk. It is but one half of the curse. The lesser half, in fact. The two really guilty ones have yet to die, the murderous Sathynarayan and the rascally car-driver who helped him.'

194

It is a rare thing for an Indian to confide his innermost thoughts to a man of Western origin. An unwritten and unspoken proscription exists against persons of another race and colour, to whom it is considered most unwise to impart secret information of any importance. There is a general belief that Westerners are extremely foolish, very callous, most disbelieving and, in fact, grossly ignorant of all matters not directly involving the five material senses. This prejudice is everywhere in the land and perhaps strongest in the minds of simple folk from the villages and jungles. It took me more than two hours of subtle and adroit questioning before I could wheedle from the old man the facts which I have already set forth in this story. Considering moreover, that I have mixed with jungle folk and villagers from the time I—and they—could walk and talk, I consider myself extremely lucky to have been able to get all the facts I eventually collected.

To me, of course, all this was but jungle-talk, the sort of thing one could expect to hear from superstitious folk. In my opinion, the tiger was just a tiger and nothing more. Perhaps it was a wounded animal and in pain when it saw the woman and child and attacked them in sheer rage. Maybe the crying of the child attracted and enticed it, perhaps even annoyed it. Maybe a hundred other reasons, but it was only a flesh-and-blood tiger. From this followed the next thought that, although for some unaccountable reason it had not eaten either of its victims, it might attack again at any time. Accordingly I made arrangements to try to shoot it. At that time I was not working, so the time factor did not count and I was in not hurry to return to city life.

As I have related in other books, most man-eaters follow a regular 'beat' in the territory where they operate. By this I mean that they follow a definite itinerary in moving from one jungle area to another, past particular villages, up the beds of or across certain streams, or along certain game-trails and fire-lines, in moving from one locality to another. Having moved this way once and killed and eaten a human or two here and there, they come back along the same trails and routes after a certain period of time, and do this over and over again. So, with patience and care, it is possible to map out the 'beat' followed by such a man-eater and to forecast with considerable accuracy when and where to wait for him in ambush, or try to entice him with a bait or by some other means.

All this did not apply in the present case. This animal had not killed any other human being anywhere for miles around. As I have said, it had not even attacked a single cow in any of the herds, nor had it killed a deer or pig as far as was known.

I enlisted the aid of the poojarees and herdsmen in the *patti* and scoured the bed of the Chinar river, both up and down, for several miles in each direction in order to find its pug-marks and ascertain if it was a male or female. Search as we did, we found no pug-marks anywhere.

This tiger must have come from the east, therefore, where lay comparatively open country, scrub jungle which petered out into cultivation for miles around. No tiger could live, or conceal itself, in such conditions. It had to come from the forest. Tigers do not live in fields!

I prevailed upon the herdsmen to lend me four cattle from the herd that belonged to Sathynarayan's father, promising to pay for any one that was killed. I knew that the owner would not object under the circumstances, but nonetheless sent one of the herdsmen to Dharamapuri to inform the owner of what I was doing.

I found the poojarees in the *patti* disinclined to be cooperative in the proceedings from this point onwards. The

ancient one among them told me, flatly that I could not expect
him and his clan-members to help me to lay a trap for their
dead companion when he turned up in the form of a tiger—
not that he would be so foolish as to kill any of the baits I
had tied up, or allow himself to be shot at. It was well known
that no bullet made of lead could penetrate a spirit.
Nevertheless, it was the motive of their actions in helping me
by which they would be judged. They could not, and would
not assist me in trying to shoot this tiger.

Money talks and so I was able to entice the herdsmen who
were not poojarees to aid me. After much inquiring and
tramping up and down, I chose four places as being the most
likely for a tiger to turn up. All that I could do now was to
wait complacently till one of the baits was taken.

Rather than be idle meanwhile, I scoured the forest from
dawn to dusk searching for the pugs of the tiger up and down
the banks of the Chinar river. As the herdsmen and poojarees
at Panapatti were not keen on helping me, I sent for my old
friend Byra, himself a poojaree, who lived at Anaibiddahalla,
another *patti* about fifteen miles distant, and for Ranga who
had accompanied me on many adventures. Both these men
were expert trackers and knew the area for miles around. But
the three of us searched in vain: not a single tiger-pug did
we find. The killer had disappeared as silently and as suddenly
as he had come.

Time ran out on me and the day came to go back to
Bangalore. I returned the four baits I had borrowed together
with a small gratuity. Normally, it is not possible to come
to an arrangement of this sort and the hunter is compelled
to purchase his baits outright. But this case was an exception
because they knew for certain hat none of the baits would
be harmed. How could they, when there was no tiger to
harm them?

About two months elapsed and Das, the driver, was returning alone to Dharamapuri in the big family car from the city of Salem, sixty-five miles away, where he had taken Sathynarayan's father for admission to hospital for removal of a cataract. Das had left the old man there and was hurrying back for dinner. He had forty miles to go to reach his home in Dharamapuri. The road narrowed down to traverse the winding bund of a large deep tank. There appeared to be no traffic in sight and Das accelerated.

Then something must have happened to the steering, or may be a front tyre blew out. Nobody knows for certain. The only witnesses were two villagers hurrying homewards who saw the whole incident. The car left the roadway suddenly at a point where the road turned left, crashed through the thin brick wall bordering the bund directly ahead and plunged headlong into the tank.

Das had closed the windows. He was trapped in the car and his body was recovered a week later when the vehicle was hauled out by the police.

Was it coincidence that he was drowned in the very tank into which he had thrown the body of Kaiyara after his master and he had murdered the poojaree and weighted the body with a stone? Sathynarayan heard the news and madness fell upon him. First, his only son, then his wife. Now the chauffeur, Das.

Sathynarayan remembered the murder of the old poojaree and his daughter before him. Tales had been carried to him about the curse the old man had uttered against him and he became convinced it was his turn next. At that moment, Sathynarayan realized he must die. Thus his mind gave way. His father returned from hospital to find his son a lunatic. The old man did not spare expense. He took Sathynarayan to Salem and consulted the best of doctors. The boy kept repeating the names of Kaiyara and Mardee in his raving but the doctors could do nothing to cure him.

Sathynarayan was then taken to Madras, and admitted to a mental home. The psychiatrist discovered that the mania arose from some connection in the madman's mind with the two persons whose names he kept muttering. However, no treatment was effective and the father became reconciled to the fact that his son and heir was permanently insane. The young man was brought home, where he was given two male attendants to look after him night and day. His father hoped that he would improve with time.

In this he was doomed to disappointment. His son became worse and grew violent, whereas before he had been but a gibbering maniac. The old man reluctantly decided that he would have to put him into the asylum at Madras as a permanent inmate. But this was not to be, for the curse of Kaiyara had yet to exact its full toll—or so people said!

Sathynarayan was missing from his room when his attendant brought his breakfast early one morning. He had been there the evening before. A search was made all over the town but nobody remembered to have seen him anywhere. They young man was well known and somebody would have noticed his movements. It was four days later when vultures spiralled the sky above the track that leads from the main road to the cattle kraal at Panapatti. They flew in wide circles, which narrowed as the birds of prey rapidly increased in numbers. Then, one after another, they plummetted to earth, their wing-feathers emitting a loud rattling noise as they tore through the air.

Byra saw the vultures and heard the sound. He had taken employment that year among the graziers at Panapatti and was driving a herd of cattle to the forest for grazing. He knew the vultures had spotted a 'kill', and being a hunter from childhood he went to investigate. Perhaps there might be some meat for him to eat.

The kill was easy to find. The discordant screeching noise made by the vultures led him to it unerringly. The birds were gathered round in a circle and had not yet begun to feed. For they were afraid!

The reason for that fear lay in the fact that dead thing they were contemplating was a human body. It was Sathynarayan, and he had been killed by a tiger. But no part of his flesh had been eaten.

Byra told me, the next time we met, that he and the other poojarees and herdsmen had searched the whole area thoroughly for pug-marks, but they had found none. Then he shrugged: 'How could we *dorai*?' he asked. 'For it was no tiger that killed that swine! Kaiyara made a good job of it.'

Printed in Great Britain
by Amazon

55000221R00122